Just a Cowboy's Enemy

Flyboys of Sweet Briar Ranch in North Dakota

Book Three

Jessie Gussman

Published By: Jessie Gussman

Written by Jessie Gussman.

Contents

Acknowledgments

Cover art by Julia Gussman
Editing by Heather Hayden
Narration by Jay Dyess
Author Services by CE Author Assistant

Listen to a FREE professionally performed and produced audiobook version of this title on Youtube. Search for "Say With Jay" to browse all available FREE Dyess/Gussman audiobooks.

Chapter 1

"I would prefer not to be in the kissing booth."

Brooklyn Lepley knew her words were not nearly strong enough. She should have said firmly, *I will not do the kissing booth.*

But it was always so hard to look into Miss Charlene's eyes and turn her down for anything. Mostly because she knew Miss Charlene would do anything for Brooklyn. And had.

When their oldest sister Cheyenne had been dying of cancer, the ladies of the town had rallied around their family, cooking meals, taking turns helping out at the house, cleaning, driving, getting the kids off to school, helping with homework, even making sure the ranch kept running.

They had fundraisers multiple times over the years to help with hospital bills and co-pays and expenses.

Brooklyn looked down at the floor.

Cheyenne hadn't made it, but part of Cheyenne's legacy was how it had taught Brooklyn that being a part of a community was not something that a person took for granted.

Part of not taking that for granted was pulling her weight, whatever she needed to.

Even if it meant being in the kissing booth for the annual Sweet Water Summer Festival.

Except, she just couldn't do it.

Miss Charlene sighed but didn't look like she was judging her or even upset. She simply looked at Miss April sadly, and said, "The kissing booth is usually our biggest moneymaker, but it's the one thing I always have trouble getting people to do. I guess... I guess we just won't have it this year."

Her eyes seemed to slide to Brooklyn's, and if it were anyone other than Miss Charlene, Brooklyn would have said that there was some kind of calculating thought in her gaze, but it just couldn't be.

Miss April said, "That's too bad. And we were going to send the proceeds of the kissing booth to the Fargo Children's Cancer Memorial Hospital." Miss Charlene and Miss April sadly shook their heads. Brooklyn might have been imagining it, but she almost thought that Miss Helen and Miss June each wiped a tear from the corner of their eye.

She almost crossed her arms over her chest and accused the ladies of laying it on really thick, because they were making her feel guilty.

They didn't have to say Cheyenne's name in order to make Brooklyn feel like she owed the town a lot more than two hours in the kissing booth. The problem was, she knew, without a shadow of a doubt, who she would be in the kissing booth with.

Cormac.

There was no way she was going to be in the kissing booth with Cormac. She refused.

Miss April lifted her head, and either she had something stuck in her eye, or they were watering.

Brooklyn tried to tell herself they weren't watering.

"If you change your mind, go ahead and let us know. But otherwise, we just won't be able to do it this year."

Brooklyn tried to steel her heart. She wasn't going to be persuaded into spending two hours with Cormac just because the ladies made her feel guilty and also because of Cheyenne's memory shimmering in the back of her head, seeming to tell her that life was not about making herself happy or about being selfish.

"All right, I'll do it." She closed her eyes, the words coming out quickly before she changed her mind. Or before she walked out.

If the ladies were anyone else, they might have said something along the lines, "No. You said you weren't, and we know you don't want to, so don't worry about it."

But that's not what the ladies did.

Miss Charlene clapped her hands, and Miss April said immediately, "Thank you very much. We'll put your name down. I know there's going to be a big crowd this year, and this will be huge."

Yeah. People always came if they knew that Brooklyn and Cormac were going to be together.

They both had been assigned to the kissing booth three years ago, but Cormac had mysteriously developed double pneumonia right in the middle of summer. Funny, because she had seen him the week before the festival and the week after, and he looked healthy as a horse both times.

She could only surmise that the reason he hadn't gone to the summer festival, and had backed out of the kissing booth, was because he didn't want to be with her.

Well, the feeling was mutual. Plus, she was the one with all the grievances.

"We don't want to keep you. You go ahead and do what you were planning on doing. Delivering groceries or something, right?" Miss Charlene said, almost as though she knew Brooklyn was on the verge of changing her mind and telling them she wouldn't do it and wanted to show her out the door before she could.

That was probably a good strategy. As long as it had taken Brooklyn to actually get here with the intention of telling them she couldn't, she'd never make it back in before the festival started.

And unlike some people, once she said she would do something, she would do it, unless there was a very good reason why she wouldn't.

She wouldn't make up some ridiculous explanation like double pneumonia.

"Yeah. I was delivering groceries to Mrs. Reinhart."

Maybe her voice sounded a little fatalistic. Like she knew her goose was cooked and there was nothing she could do about it.

After all, the shimmering picture of Cheyenne in the back of her head wouldn't allow her to open her mouth and tell these ladies that she wasn't going to do the most profitable thing at the summer festival, wasn't going to allow them to make money to send to the Fargo Children's Cancer Memorial Hospital, wasn't going to pay back the town for everything they had done for them over the years.

Of course she was going to do it.

Even if she had to hold her nose the entire time.

As well she might, since she didn't know how else she was going to get through two hours in the kissing booth with Cormac Henderson.

She waved at the ladies as she walked out the door, still a little upset that they manipulated her into doing what they wanted her to do, but knowing she would never hold a grudge.

She was well aware that the ladies had a reputation for matchmaking, but Miss Charlene had seemed to retire after her marriage to Charlie, and while the Piece Makers still met in the basement of the church, it wasn't the same.

Things changed, people moved on, and that was life.

Miss April, along with Miss Helen and Miss June, met at the community center to do crafts, and rumor had it, they talked about how to have good marriages and be good wives.

Miss Charlene dropped in once in a while to add her wisdom to the discussion.

They were no longer matchmaking.

She almost laughed at that idea. Because if they were, they were totally wasting their time on her and Cormac. There was no future in matchmaking for anyone who thought that was a good match.

It was a beautiful day out, and she decided she wasn't going to drive her car down the street to Mrs. Reinhart's house but simply grab the groceries out of the back and walk them down.

As she rooted around in the trunk, she realized she had underestimated the number of groceries she had bought.

There were ten bags, which she could easily hold in each hand, but there was also a box of tissues and a large twelve-roll package of paper towels.

With five bags in each hand, a box in one, and the paper towels in the other, she would look ridiculous as she walked down the street, but she'd already decided she wasn't driving, so she hefted the things up, balancing the paper towels with the side of her head and the box of tissues with her chin.

She nodded at her sister Teagan and her new husband, Deuce, whom she passed as they walked into the diner. They commented on what a beautiful morning it was, and she concurred.

"Do you need help with those?" Teagan asked as Deuce held the door open for her.

"No. I'm exercising." She grinned, to make her statement a fun one rather than looking like she was struggling. It really was good exercise, although she hadn't deliberately set out for that reason.

Still, she loved the challenge, and she definitely was going to make it. The bags were heavy but not unbearable, and it would feel good to get everything there in one load. Challenging herself to do something a little bit hard.

Maybe she'd missed the fact that one of the bags had a hole in it, or maybe the weight from the cans of diced tomatoes was too much for the plastic, but she had barely taken another fifty steps toward Mrs. Reinhart's house when one of the bags broke, the cans spilling out and rolling down the sidewalk.

She'd been pretty confident not two minutes before, now she was kicking herself.

Using her feet, she tried to stop all the cans from rolling toward the road, since she could hear a truck rumbling down Main Street behind her.

It wouldn't be coming fast, nothing went fast through Sweet Water, but she didn't want to lose any of her cans, if she could help it.

Allowing the box of tissues and the paper towels to drop to the ground, she let go of the bags in one hand and ran after one can that must have hit a hill or slope in the sidewalk since it was going faster than all the other ones and was on a diagonal to drop off the edge of the sidewalk and onto the road.

Thankfully, the truck passed before the can dropped.

Maybe her concentration was a little bit off, or maybe she wasn't as coordinated as she used to be, but as she got close to the can, with her fingers just a few inches from it, she ended up kicking it with her foot, so it sailed off in an arc and landed in the middle of the street.

By that time, she was going too fast to stop, and she ran out after it.

Foolishly, it turned out, since the Highlander cow that had been running loose in Sweet Water since last winter was apparently following the truck.

Maybe the truck was hauling feed or something. She wasn't sure why the cow would be chasing it, but she hadn't heard its hooves pounding on the pavement until it was too late.

Well, not quite too late, since strong arms wrapped around her and lifted her off her feet, swinging her to the left.

Just in time, since the Highlander's fur brushed her arm as it went past.

She wasn't quite sure how the horns missed them, but they did.

Maybe it was a tension relief, but she laughed a little as her feet settled back on the sidewalk and she turned, a smile on her face and words of appreciation on her lips for whoever had been more aware of her surroundings than she was and had rescued her from being run over by a cow.

That would be something she would never live down in a small town. She would always be known as that girl who had gotten run over by a cow and ended up in the hospital for three days with broken ribs and lacerations from the encounter.

The joke about saving her reputation died on her lips as she saw just who had rescued her.

Cormac Henderson.

Chapter 2

Cormac Henderson walked to the door of the diner on his way out and met Teagan and Deuce on their way in.

"Good morning," he said, nodding his head at the couple who was finally a couple, if the rumors around town were to be believed. After years of neither one of them realizing how perfect they were for each other, they were finally together.

Deuce and he had been friends from way back, and he had mentioned once or twice over the years to Deuce that he and Teagan should be more.

Apparently, Deuce had either taken his advice, or Teagan had taken matters into her own hands, but whatever it was, he was glad to see them, because they were perfect together.

"Good morning, Cormac. Your favorite person just walked by and could use a hand carrying some groceries."

Cormac didn't have any trouble figuring out who Deuce was talking about. People always referred to Brooklyn Lepley as his favorite person or that person he secretly loved, or sometimes, people came right out and called her his enemy.

He wasn't sure exactly what had happened when they'd been in school, but he regretted it. Brooklyn wasn't exactly the kind of person a man could just go up to and explain that he made a mistake, then ask her what the mistake was. She'd been humiliated, he'd figured that much out, and she'd probably never talk to him again.

It bothered him, but it wasn't like he had been in love with her or anything, although to be honest, she had attracted his eye more than any other girl ever had. But his heart wasn't broken, and she had retaliated in a not very nice way, and if people said she wasn't his favorite person, they were speaking the truth.

They might have patched up their differences a few years ago when they were supposed to be in the kissing booth together at the Sweet Water Summer Festival.

If only that bout of double pneumonia hadn't kept him from participating.

He hadn't been extremely sick, the antibiotics that the doctor had given him had kicked the pneumonia out pretty fast, but the idea of forcing someone to kiss him when he still had some head cold-type drainage was just disgusting.

Especially considering the shaky ground that Brooklyn and he had always been on together.

"Maybe we should stand here and talk a little bit," he joked, gratified when Deuce's eyes crinkled.

"Or maybe you should just hurry out the door and patch up your differences," Teagan said, her brows raised, her head jerking toward the door that was slowly closing behind them.

"I guess I'd better show the lady I'm a gentleman," he said, figuring Teagan would be upset if Deuce stood and talked to him like Cormac would prefer. Brooklyn was not going to appreciate his help, so he could go offer it if he wanted to, but he knew her answer would be no.

Still, if she saw him make the effort... That probably wouldn't make a difference, either.

"Which way did she go?" he asked, like he was going to go that way. But he planned to turn the exact opposite.

"Left."

"Right."

Deuce and Teagan looked at each other, Teagan acting like she was trying to tell Deuce something, and Deuce looking completely clueless.

Their voices had been so well blended together that he wasn't sure which one had said which way, but he guessed that Teagan had told him the wrong way, and Deuce had told him the right way. Or maybe Teagan didn't want him to tangle with Brooklyn. He wasn't sure. At any rate, they were no help, and he just shook his head, laughing as he pushed the door open and walked out.

A truck passed in front of the diner, which wasn't too unusual, considering there was a feed mill and trucking garage at one end of Sweet Water and an auction barn at the other end. Loads of feed ingredients, along with stock feed, bulk feed, and various types of animals went through town all the time.

Everyone was used to it.

What really drew his eye was movement to his left, as someone, he gave himself one guess as to who, although he couldn't tell because her back was to him, bent down, one arm flailing like she'd lost her balance, one arm reaching out in front of her to try to grab a can that rolled down the sidewalk just out of her reach.

Bags littered the sidewalk behind her, along with some type of box and what looked like a bulk roll of toilet paper or maybe paper towels.

He narrowed his eyes.

Surely she heard the truck coming and wasn't going to run out in front of it.

But he knew how he was when he got focused on completing a task. Sometimes the things that were going on around him faded into the background.

Just as he thought that, the truck rolled down beside her, and while she was still careening toward the edge of the sidewalk, it wasn't close to her at all.

But that's when he just happened to look slightly to his right and see the Highlander cow that had been running loose in Sweet Water for not quite a year running down the road, ostensibly after the truck.

If Brooklyn didn't hear the truck, she almost assuredly wouldn't hear the cow.

The thought sped through his mind, and in a second, maybe less, he came to the conclusion that if he didn't do something, Brooklyn was going to get plowed over by the Highlander cow.

Not because the cow was mean. On the contrary, he'd seen upwards of eight or ten kids all with their hands buried in its fur while it stood still, seeming to love the attention.

But it did seem to have a singleness of purpose; its infatuation with the pig that ran around town being case in point.

Hopefully, the cow had not decided it was a truck and had fallen in love with an inanimate object. Trying to explain to outsiders why the cow chased the pig around was hard enough.

If he had to start trying to explain why it chased trucks...that might be a lot harder.

Regardless, he took off at a dead sprint toward Brooklyn.

They might have a rocky history, and she might not be his favorite person, and he knew she hated him, but he still couldn't stand around while someone got plowed over, if there was anything he could do to prevent it.

He reached her just ahead of the Highlander, grabbed her, and swung her back.

Just in time, since he felt the fur of the creature, who didn't even seem to slow down as it ran by them, brush his arm.

Yeah. He basically just saved her life. Or at the very least saved her from the embarrassment of being that woman who got run over by the cow for the rest of her life, and possibly a stay in the hospital. If this didn't solve the animosity that lay between them, nothing would.

She glanced up at the cow and then turned toward him, a grin on her face and gratefulness in her eyes.

Yeah. He could be gracious, allow her to grovel a little, apologize for being mean to him all those years, and thank him for deciding to rescue her despite the fact that she'd never been kind, at least not in the last ten or so years.

If that's what he thought she was going to say, and it really was, he was disappointed.

"You," she spat out, like he had shoved poison ivy in her mouth instead of saving her life from the charging cow.

He lifted his hands and looked around. "No one else was running to your rescue." He should just keep his mouth shut, a little voice inside of his mind reminded him, but he couldn't. "And I guess I know why."

Her eyes got big, and any gratitude or humor that had been on her face was completely gone. Her eyes narrowed. "Because it's a small town, and there wasn't anyone on the street. I'm sure you're not insinuating anything else."

"I wasn't insinuating anything. I'll come right out and say it. No one wanted to rescue you."

"Maybe I didn't want you to rescue me. Maybe I didn't need to be rescued. Maybe I preferred that you never touch me again."

"Wow. Our first conversation in eleven and a half years, not that I'm keeping track, and it went pretty much the way I expected it to after the way you behaved."

"Me?" Her eyes blinked like they refused to stay open, fluttering as though they couldn't make up their mind, or maybe it was the fact that her eyeballs wanted to jump out of their sockets, and her eyelashes were flailing with the effort to keep them in.

He snorted at the idea.

His snort, if possible, made her even angrier.

That made him smile even bigger.

"Kind of feels like you might give me the opportunity to be a hero for a second time today, when I throw water on you after you spontaneously combust here in about five seconds."

Yeah, her narrowed eyes would have been shooting poison-tipped darts at him if possible, he was sure. And her jaw, clenched so hard he could see her cheek muscles twitching, clearly said he definitely made her angry.

He hadn't meant to. He had been willing to reconcile, it was her who had turned around and been mean.

You said things you knew would goad her, on purpose.

That was true. He should feel bad about that. And part of him kind of did. But he supposed there was another part of him that was still holding a grudge about the way she had reacted to whatever he had done in high school. And the fact that she'd never given him a chance to explain.

So yeah, maybe there was a little hurt there. Not that he would admit that.

"A hero? You?" Her expression showed her derision. "Actually, you were probably trying to push me in front of the cow and accidentally moved me out of the way. Now, that's a take I would believe." Her lips flattened, and she looked around. He realized she was probably looking for the can she'd been chasing when he'd first seen her.

"All right. Sorry to interrupt your...I don't even know what that was with you sticking your butt in the air and your head down to the ground like a hound dog on the trail. Go ahead and keep sniffing for whatever you were looking for."

Her mouth gaped like she couldn't believe he would have said such a thing to her. But he didn't think it was that mean.

"I'm not sure what you're all upset about. Hound dogs are kinda cute, if you like furry, smelly things, and the similarities between you and them are quite apparent, to me anyway."

"Now I know why I haven't talked to you for the last eleven years. That was not nearly long enough. Do you think you feel a case of double pneumonia coming on?"

It was his turn to blink. Women had a tendency to do that, change the subject right in the middle of a sentence sometimes, and he was a little slow following.

"I can't believe you're asking about my health out of concern for my welfare, so there must be some kind of catch to that."

"Oh, there is. There's a big catch. I'm sure Miss April or Miss Charlene is going to be talking to you. You better start coughing now, practice up."

She sounded a little bitter, almost as though she resented the fact that he had gotten sick. Like he wanted to.

He supposed it was possible, after he thought about it for a couple of seconds, that she thought that he had backed out of being in the kissing booth by using that as an excuse, and he hadn't really been sick.

"I suppose you want to see my doctor's excuse." He couldn't keep from smirking. After all, he had been telling the truth, and she didn't believe him, and he knew it.

"Really? You went to the trouble of forging a doctor's excuse for yourself? Or are you only going to do that if I demand to see it?" Some of the heat had gone out of her words, like she was tired of fighting.

Her reputation around town, other than with him, was kind and sweet and gentle. He seemed to bring out the worst in her. The same as she did to him.

It was probably just as well that they avoided each other. He hadn't been kind, and maybe he should apologize... Yeah. Since he wasn't planning on talking to her for the next decade or so, it wouldn't hurt to leave with an apology.

He opened his mouth, when a blur in his peripheral vision caught his attention and he turned his head.

That cow, the one that had been chasing the truck down the street, Billy, he thought the town had named him, had emerged from between two parked cars across the street and was heading straight toward them.

He hadn't heard of Billy charging anyone, or hurting anyone for that matter, other than putting a small hole in Smith's T-shirt, and that was a matter of speculation, since even Smith admitted that the T-shirt might have had a hole in it before Billy brushed by him.

There hadn't been a mark on his body, and no one had ever been hurt in any other incidents.

But while all that ran through his head in a split second, and it all sounded reasonable, the fact of the matter was, the cow was charging at them now.

Not at him. At Brooklyn.

Part of him was tempted to just let it go. After all, she had said he wasn't a hero.

But he couldn't.

"Looks like the cow's coming back." He nodded in that direction, sounding a lot calmer than what he felt.

In just another second, he would reach out and grab Brooklyn, but he didn't need to because she saw the cow's trajectory, knew she was in its way, and keeping her eyes on the charging animal, took two long steps forward, which made her plow into his arms.

He caught her automatically, swung her around again, and this time, the cow didn't even brush them as it ran by.

"Did you do something to offend it?" he asked, meaning it as a joke, but of course she didn't take it that way.

Maybe he'd forgotten who he was holding. She was soft, with curves in the right places, and she smelled unique and amazing, like strawberries and laughter, and there was a part of his brain that didn't want to let her go.

Maybe it was his imagination, but she seemed to stand in his arms for a second or two longer than necessary.

Or maybe it was just relief from having almost gotten run over twice in the last fifteen minutes.

"Maybe it has been talking to you. That's all I can figure out," she muttered as she backed up, shaking her head.

She didn't even look at him, didn't thank him, but walked over to where her can rested against the tire of the car that was parked ten feet down the sidewalk.

She bent down and grabbed it and walked over to the mess that was still scattered all over the sidewalk from where she had been dropping things when she chased the cans that had fallen out of the broken bag.

No one else had walked down the sidewalk, or someone would have helped her pick them up.

Looking up and down the street, he could see everything was still deserted. Even the cow, wherever it had come from, had disappeared again.

Knowing she wasn't going to appreciate it, he followed her over to the sidewalk, bending down and picking up three cans, then standing as she straightened.

He wasn't sure where she wanted them, and he knew better than to just stick them in a bag. Women could be touchy about their groceries.

And while he might not like this woman very much, he still didn't want to offend her by putting her cans in the wrong bag.

He waited, but she acted like he wasn't there.

"That's mature," he said dryly. Irritated for some unreasonable reason that he had saved her—twice—and she couldn't even bring herself to say thank you but instead was ignoring him, like high school had been two days ago instead of more than a decade.

"What?" she asked, still picking things up and putting them in a bag or at least pretending to be busy with movements. After all, he hadn't seen that much stuff still sitting on the sidewalk, but she was effectively ignoring him.

"I'm trying to hand you the cans I picked up for you, and you're ignoring me. That's mature."

"Oh. I'm sorry. I'm not acting the way you want me to. I suppose you're going to lie about me to the entire town now and not just the school. Well, go right ahead. You can set the cans down. I'll get them when I'm ready."

He hadn't lied about her to the whole school. But he figured there was no point in arguing about it or even trying to defend himself. It was obvious she wasn't willing to listen to the truth.

It irritated him to walk away without contradicting what she said, but he put the cans down.

Maybe he hadn't completely realized what she thought. That she thought the rumors that had gone around school were started by him.

They hadn't been.

It was obvious she believed they had, though. No wonder she had been so mad at him for so long.

He stood, the cans on the sidewalk in front of him, his hands in his pockets.

If she had given the slightest bit of a signal that she might be willing to put the past behind them, he would explain.

But the way she was acting now made it obvious that whatever he said, she wasn't going to actually hear him.

And that was too bad, because he thought she was probably a pretty nice person.

But after the way she treated him today, maybe it was just as well that he kept his distance from her.

Without saying anything more, he turned and walked away.

Chapter 3

"Would you rather he let you fall to the ground?" Cassie smiled, trying to hide the humor in her heart, although she knew it came out in her voice a little.

"No. Of course not." Brooklyn held the door while Cassie walked through carrying the tray of vegetables and water to the porch.

In the summer, the porch was her favorite place to be. And anytime she had visitors, she tried to take them outside if she could.

There was a small area that was not under a roof, so they could sit in the sun in the spring and fall and let the sun warm them.

Today was one of those days, right at the end of May, where sitting in the sun felt good and not too hot.

"So you're saying I shouldn't be complaining." Brooklyn's expression showed that she knew she was complaining about something she shouldn't be but just couldn't help it.

"I didn't say that," Cassie said immediately. She wanted to be a good friend, and sometimes that meant commiserating with someone when things really weren't fair. Although, a lot of the time she found herself commiserating, then reminding people that whatever God gave them was the best thing for them.

Maybe people were just being polite, since she had cancer, and there weren't too many people who could talk like that. So if she said cancer was something God gave her and was the best thing for her, people really couldn't argue.

Still, she didn't want to not be compassionate. Sometimes things that seemed small and inconsequential to one person felt like the end of the world to another. And Cassie knew just how much Brooklyn didn't care for Cormac.

She had been there when he'd treated Brooklyn the way he had. She'd heard the rumors at school and had seen Brooklyn's heartrending tears.

She'd known how hard it was for Brooklyn to pull herself up and walk into school with her head held high.

She'd even listened as Brooklyn had said she wanted to quit school and run away. Not wanting to face the jeers and teasing of her classmates.

Maybe that was something that a lot of people went through.

"If you could change what happened in high school, would you?" Cassie waited until Brooklyn lifted her eyes after she set the tray down.

"Of course I would! That was the worst time of my life!" Brooklyn eyed Cassie before she put several carrots and some broccoli florets on her plate.

"But what you learned through that experience shaped you into the person you became. Don't you think there was some good?"

Brooklyn's lips flattened, but there was a little bit of a smile at the corners. "I know. Being teased in high school isn't as bad as having cancer."

"I wasn't saying that. I was asking sincerely. When I look back over my life, it's the hard times that were really where my relationship with the Lord grew. I had to draw closer to Him and had to depend on Him more and more. I...definitely didn't appreciate it at the time, and I never for one second would think to thank God for cancer or for not getting the big-name job I applied for out of college. At the time. But I appreciate it now. And I'm thankful."

She didn't want her words to sound like she was lecturing Brooklyn, because she wasn't. People responded to things in different ways. Cassie had just lived her life, despite the things she couldn't control, and had decided she was going to respond in the best way she could.

"Don't get me wrong. You know I'm not perfect."

"It feels like you're perfect. You're right, that having cancer has made you a more spiritual person. I know if I need advice, I can come here and you will tell me what the Bible says. There aren't a lot of places I can go where I can say that."

"I spent a lot of time on the couch, listening to the Bible when I couldn't read it." Those had been hard times. For sure. But like she had just told Brooklyn, they'd made her stronger. "I just meant that sometimes I struggle too. I question God. I don't want to do what I know He wants me to. Sometimes I can't even tell what that is. Sometimes I'm not sure whether what I want to do is what He wants me to do or just something I really want to do and I'm not listening to Him about. You know?"

"You have always been perfect in your walk."

"Well, maybe looks can be deceiving, or maybe I should be more careful to make sure people can see that I'm not perfect."

"No. I don't think anyone thinks you're a hypocrite."

"Well, sometimes I wake up in the middle of the night and I feel a little twinge, and I wonder, is the cancer back? Sometimes fear feels like a plastic bag over my head or a couple of heavy bricks on my chest, just pushing me down, making it so I can't breathe, and I feel like I'm dying, when I know I'm just afraid."

"How do you handle that?" Brooklyn asked, tilting her head like she had never once considered that Cassie might face fear.

She'd had cancer, for goodness' sake. Of course she was afraid.

"Well, I know that the spirit of fear is not from God. The Bible says that God gives us a sound mind, not a spirit of fear. So I knew it was the devil. I know it's wrong to be afraid. God tells us over and over to fear not."

"You can't just tell yourself not to be afraid," Brooklyn said.

"No. I guess not."

"You do that?" Brooklyn asked, a carrot held in midair.

"I guess. Kind of. The Bible says that the devil flees from Jesus's name. So I call out to Jesus. I tell him I don't want to be afraid. And then I guess I kind of reason with myself."

"Like you talk to yourself?"

"Yeah, kind of." It hadn't occurred to her that people might be interested in what she had learned to do. She just figured people would think she was crazy if she told them. "I... I say, what's the worst thing that could happen?"

"You could die!" Brooklyn said like that was truly the worst thing that could happen.

"Isn't the worst thing that could happen is that I could go to hell?"

"Yeah," she finally said after she thought about it for a moment. "I guess that would be worse than dying."

"That's what happened to me. I'm saved from the worst thing. Now, there are a lot of other things that I can reason with myself about, once I realized that the worst thing that could happen, that I can go to hell, isn't going to happen."

"Okay?"

"I'll say to myself, if everything works out for good to those who love God, whatever happens, whatever this thing is I'm afraid of, the outcome is going to work out for good. God isn't going to allow me to go through anything that He doesn't want me to. So if He wants me to fall off of a bridge, it doesn't matter how I avoid bridges, I'm going to fall off of one. And if He doesn't want me to, I won't. It's just not going to happen."

"Okay, and that works?"

"It does for me. To know that if I die, I'm going to heaven, and I'm going to be a lot happier there than I am here. That takes a little of the sting of death away. Like the Bible says, death was swallowed up in victory. I don't have to be afraid of it anymore. Even though, as humans, it's something that is intrinsic in our makeup. Because of course, we're supposed to live until God's ready for us to die."

"Okay, that makes sense. Death shouldn't be our biggest fear."

"No. Of course not. And a lot of times, that's what my fear is at night. I don't even articulate it. I just wake up afraid. I'll feel a twinge, or a little pain, and wonder if that's cancer, and it just makes me scared. But I have to trust in the goodness of God."

"Sometimes I'm not sure God's good," Brooklyn admitted, almost as though she were ashamed of it.

"Then maybe that's something you can work on when you're not afraid. I did that a lot. I made myself think about all the things that God does that are good. All of His promises. I meditated on those. Read them through every day. Wrote some down. And just kept telling myself that God is good. He's merciful. He loves me and doesn't want anything bad to happen to me." Cassie put some dip on her plate and then absently ran a carrot through it. "I think, it's easier to run to God when you're scared, if you know Him. And you need to know Him before you get to the point where you need Him. Does that make sense? Just like a little kid doesn't run to just any adult that they don't know, they run to their parents, whom they love and trust. That's us. We need to develop a relationship with Him so it's natural to run to Him, because we love Him and trust Him and know He loves us."

"I've never seen things that way. That makes a lot of sense. I need to know God and love Him and trust Him in order for Him to be able to calm my fear and make me feel safe."

Brooklyn seemed like she was thinking about what she'd said, and Cassie didn't say anything more. Brooklyn hadn't come here to talk about Cassie's fears.

After they'd eaten for a little while without saying anything, Cassie gently tried to change the subject.

"We were talking about your meeting with Cormac."

Brooklyn laughed. "It wasn't a meeting. It was a catastrophe."

"But he caught you!" Cassie said, her head tilted, humor in her eyes.

"All right. He gets a little credit for that, but seriously, I think I'd have been just as happy if he would have ignored me and just let me fall to the ground while he walked on by."

"And if that would have happened, you would be sitting here right now complaining about what a rude person he was for not catching you and for not even asking if you were okay."

Brooklyn huffed out a breath. "You're right. And that would have been much more satisfying to me—"

"And totally suit your narrative."

"If that would have happened. And you're right. It would be much more in line with what I want to believe about Cormac."

"So, the actual Cormac isn't the wicked man you believe him to be?"

"Why do you have to be so wise? I don't want to hear wisdom like that. I want to hear you tell me that he's a jerk and I'm right and that there are no redemptive qualities in him at all."

"People are very seldom all good or all bad." Cassie thought again about what Brooklyn had said about her, thinking that she was some kind of paragon of Christian piety. Which couldn't be further from the truth. Her flaws were huge mountains in her eyes, while the good things she might do were very small in comparison. Plus, she knew her heart was wicked and usually selfish. A lot of times, the good things she did, she might mean them for good, but she might also be inspired by selfish motives.

Of course, she needed to remember what she had just told Brooklyn. People were not all bad or all good, and God knew them. He didn't expect anyone's motives to be pure all the time, with no mistakes. That was what grace was for.

But she didn't want to take advantage of God's grace or act like His sacrifice didn't mean anything. So therefore, she would try as hard as she could to do right and trust God to give her grace when she did not succeed.

"You're right," Brooklyn whispered, and she looked guilty.

"Is there something you want to say?" Cassie asked gently.

"Not really. I don't want to say anything. But I wasn't very nice. It felt good at the time. I guess... I want to hurt him as badly as he hurt me. Worse. I want to win, as though it were a competition to see who could be the very worst. But that's a terrible competition, isn't it? And that's not the kind of person I want to be."

"Me either. But if cancer were a person, I'd like to have beat him up a few times."

"That's a little different."

"It's still pain, isn't it? We still want to retaliate, even though God wants us to accept things, the good and the bad, and trust Him. Cancer, people who aren't so kind, or anything in between."

Brooklyn twisted the broccoli floret that was in her hand. "Even though we want to retaliate, that doesn't mean it's okay for us to do so."

"Of course."

"And even though it's natural, it doesn't make it right."

"That's right too."

"I probably should apologize."

Cassie ducked her head to keep Brooklyn from seeing the smile on her face. It was sweet to see Brooklyn knowing that she hadn't done something the way she should and, instead of trying to justify herself, admitting that she had been wrong, and saying she should apologize.

"I think that would probably be something that would please the Lord. God says He resists the proud but gives grace to the humble. It definitely takes a big person to apologize."

"And it's definitely hardest to be humble to the people that we like the least."

"That is true. For sure."

"Maybe I won't seek him out, but if I see him again, if he will even talk to me, because I was pretty rude, I'll have to apologize."

"Sweet Water's a small town. I'm sure you'll be seeing him again."

"Actually, I'm sure I will be too. That's part of what I came here to talk to you about. The summer festival."

"I heard the rumors," Cassie said casually, unable to believe that she actually forgot about them the whole time they were talking.

"About the kissing booth?"

"Yeah. You and Cormac."

"That might have something to do with why I was acting the way I was. I don't think he has any clue. But I can't believe that they would ask me and not be asking him to do it with me. That's what everyone always does."

"Maybe the people in town see something that you guys don't." Cassie was very careful with her words. She didn't want to offend her friend. And she didn't want to tell her something that wasn't true or point her in a direction she shouldn't go.

"You're kidding, right?" Brooklyn said, the shock clear on her face.

"Not really. I mean, I think some of it is for sport, just because you guys are so funny in your dislike for each other. But...sometimes when people don't get along, it's because their personalities throw sparks. Sometimes those are good sparks."

"After what he did to me in high school, there is no way that I would ever want to have anything to do with him. I might be able to be a casual friend. Someone that, if he sees me in the grocery store, he'll stop and say hi. But nothing more. Not even a chance."

"Okay. If you say so."

"I don't like the way you said that," Brooklyn said, a smile on her face, her head tilted and her gaze quizzical. Like she was trying to figure out if Cassie knew something she didn't.

"I didn't say it any way. Not really."

"Just that you believe what you just told me."

"That people who don't get along sometimes could really get along well because their personalities throw sparks?" She nodded. "I believe that."

"What about you? Do you throw sparks with anyone?"

"Well, the town really isn't trying to get me together with anyone, are they?" She tried not to sound sad or melancholy about it. She'd accepted the fact, or at least mostly accepted, that someone with cancer wasn't exactly going to be on anyone's matchmaking list.

Even though the cancer had been declared cured, or at least in remission, she never knew when it might come back. Who wanted to gamble on a chance like that? On marrying someone and trying to build a life with them, when they might only have a few years together?

"Cassie," Brooklyn said, putting her carrot down and resting her hand on Cassie's forearm. "I'm sorry. It must be hard... I know that has to be hard, and there's not really anything I can do about it. I wish there were."

Cassie shook her head, her lips pressed together and tilted up in what she hoped was a natural-looking smile. "God knows. He has a plan for me. If it doesn't include romance...I'll be sad. Disappointed. But that's life, isn't it? We don't always get what we want. What we think we deserve. What we wish we could have. But God in His wisdom knows best."

"I wish I could surrender to God's will for my life that easily. I feel like I'm always fighting for more."

"It's not that I'm not waiting for more. I am. Who isn't? I want a lifetime love. Someone to walk beside me. Someone to hold onto in the middle of the night when I wake up scared and alone and someone to whom I can give comfort when they do too. Someone to build a life with. I... That just might not be something God has for me. And while I wish it were, and I'll keep hoping for it, I'll keep trying to keep an eye out for what God really wants for me."

"You mean, how you can be a help to other people who are single?"

"Exactly. And other cancer survivors. If they can look at me and see me smiling and happy and content with my life, maybe that will inspire them to think that they can be the same."

It wasn't exactly what she wanted, she wanted so much more in her life, but she also wanted to make God happy. And if her being single was God's plan for her, every day she would try to get up and be happy that she was in God's plan, and try not to worry about whether what she wanted was what He was giving her. Rather, she would try to make what she wanted match up with what He was giving. That was the way to a life full of contentment. Trust. Trust in God's plan that it was best.

"I suppose it's better to not be married than to be married to the wrong person."

"That's true."

"And I also suppose that it's better to be kind to people, even if you feel like they've been unkind to you. We all have our things we struggle with. No one has everything they think they want or need."

"That's so true. But I guess that's why God gave us each other. Not so we could come and have a time of complaining but rather so that we can go to each other and have each other remind ourselves of what we want to be so we can try to be more."

"That's what friends are for, isn't it?"

Cassie met Brooklyn's eyes and smiled. That was absolutely right. The best friends weren't the ones who commiserated with her but the ones who gently pushed her to be better. To be what God wanted her to be and not what she wanted.

Chapter 4

"If you think that all sounds good, I'll send a proposal over via email, and we'll pick a date in July to get started."

Cormac nodded his head and shook Jonah's hand. Then he turned to Gideon and shook his as well. Jonah had done most of the talking for the duo, and he seemed like the more serious of the two.

But Cormac got the impression that they both knew what they were talking about when it came to airplanes, and they had done their research when it came to pesticides and herbicides.

"I had to say, I'm excited about trying something new. Something that is going to be more cost-effective, and I love giving neighbors business."

That was all true. When he had heard that the men who had bought the Sweet Briar Ranch, not far from his own farm, were former Air Force men and were starting a business using airplanes and helicopters to dust crops in the area, he was hoping that their prices would be in his range and he could give them business.

He liked supporting veterans, to begin with. To pay them back a little for their service and time in service to their country. But also, he liked even more supporting neighbors.

"We weren't sure how the people around Sweet Water would feel when we came in. Sometimes it's hard for outsiders to get a footing in a small town." Jonah's eyes were just as serious as they had been the entire time he'd been talking.

Gideon, who still wore a half smile on his face, shoved his hands in his pockets and nodded.

"Sweet Water's pretty accepting. I think you'll probably always be known as those Air Force guys, or something like that."

"Miss Charlene was calling us flyboys yesterday at the diner. I think the name is going to stick. We heard it at the church too." Gideon grinned, like he liked the name, and it didn't bother him a bit.

"It seems a little old-fashioned but kinda cute."

"I don't know if cute is a good, manly description," Jonah intoned.

"Hey, if it helps us pick up chicks, I'll take it." Gideon winked.

Jonah shook his head. Cormac didn't say anything either. He wasn't real interested in picking up chicks. He wouldn't mind finding a woman, but he'd never been interested in playing the field, and that hadn't changed as he'd gotten older.

He wasn't going to discuss that with his neighbors, though. Not only because he didn't really know them, but it just wasn't something he talked about much. But he'd kind of given up. He didn't really have time, or maybe he'd just never been able to find anyone who felt compatible.

He wasn't sure. Just knew he was done wasting time dating.

"I'll look for them in my inbox. And if I hear anyone talk about flyboys, I'll know who they mean now."

Jonah and Gideon grinned, but Jonah sobered right away.

"We have an airplane, so it fits. But our efforts to get a helicopter haven't been successful so far."

"They're expensive?" Cormac asked with interest.

"That and rare. They don't make a whole lot of them, and the waiting list is pretty long. We're on it, but I was hoping we could find a good used one. So far, that hasn't worked."

"I trust God will give us what we need when we need it," Gideon said, still smiling but his words slightly more serious than the impression that he'd given up until that point.

Cormac nodded, impressed despite himself. He appreciated someone who could have fun and laugh, especially if they were able to be serious about the things that needed it. Anyone who was willing to submit to God's plan was someone he felt he could do business with.

"I'll be watching for your email. I assume you want the contract signed and sent back?"

"Yeah. I'll send it to you so you can virtually sign it. That'll negate the need to print anything off. But if you want to, you can always run the papers over if that's your thing. We're not picky." He gave a little smile. "We just appreciate the business."

"I think you'll find that the town will be happy to rally around you. Not that anybody is going to be flying in airplanes for you, but people around here want you to succeed."

"Good to know," they said in unison.

Cormac shook their hands again and walked to his pickup. Smiling.

He had been really impressed with his neighbors, who had come highly recommended by Deuce, who lived on the other side of them.

He just happened to run into Deuce and Teagan in town not that long ago and had a discussion about their new neighbors. Up until that point, Cormac hadn't realized they were setting up a business that he might be able to help with.

Thankfully it really was going to be cost-effective, since he didn't have a whole lot of cash on hand, with the drought the previous summer and the wheat blight that had decimated his crop last year.

He got in his truck and pulled out on the main highway when his phone rang.

He answered on speaker, since his truck was too old to support anything newer. It worked for him. And it kept him from having any kind of big payment which was essential for when he had slow years. Like the last few had been.

He would have enough to pay for what he had going on, but there was definitely no extra money. The expansion he had wanted to do had been put on the back burner. Or taken off the stove completely.

That was life on the farm. In good times, he tried to make up for the bad times, and in bad times, he did what he had to in order not to lose the farm. Or any livestock.

"Hello?"

"Cormac Henderson?"

"Speaking."

He didn't recognize the voice. And it hadn't registered when he glanced down at his phone to swipe it on, but thinking about it, he thought it might have had some kind of law firm on the screen.

"Cormac. This is your old college roommate, Charles."

He wouldn't have recognized him, not in a million years. He sounded...old.

"Charles. Wow. It's been a long time."

He hadn't talked to Charles since they'd graduated from college. Charles had gone on to law school, and he'd gone back to the farm. No. He'd gone to Charles's wedding. They'd talked then.

"Do you have a minute?" Charles asked.

"Sure. I've got all the time you need." He always had time for a friend. And although he had work to finish up, it could wait until he had a conversation.

"I'm dying."

Cormac blinked. It took about that long for him to decide that this might be a conversation he didn't want to have while driving. He slowed down and pulled off to the side of the road, hazard lights on.

"Whoa. You're dying?" He realized that probably wasn't the best response. "I'm sorry. That's terrible. I... What can I do?"

"I was hoping you would ask. I actually do have something I wanted you to do for me."

"Okay. I'll do anything."

"Anything?"

There was something in Charles's tone that made him think maybe he shouldn't have offered absolutely anything, but he did it without thinking.

"Of course. Whatever I can do. Just tell me."

"All right. I have a daughter. I want you to raise her for me."

"Wow. Okay." That was not what he was expecting. He thought he might have some property he wanted Cormac to take care of. Or animals he needed him to handle.

"I... Are you sure?" He had no idea how to be a father. "I'm not married. I wouldn't have a mother for her."

"My wife had someone picked out. She... She passed away in a car accident several years ago. I don't know if you heard."

"No. I didn't."

They'd seen each other at the wedding. In fact, it had been one of those instances where people had been trying to get him and Brooklyn together. That seemed to be a pastime that a lot of people had since they knew they didn't really get along with each other. Anytime they could, they stuck them together. At the wedding, they had Brooklyn and Cormac seated at the same table.

From what he understood, Brooklyn had grabbed an extra chair and sat at a table with some of her college friends.

He hadn't cared. He was happier without her, and he hadn't taken it personally. After all, if he had somewhere else to go, he would have gone.

"I didn't think so. We lost touch." The man sighed. "That's something I regret now, by the way."

"Surely there's some hope? I mean, they come up with new treatments—"

"No. I had hope for a while, but I just spoke with my doctor a few minutes ago. I... I've been fighting for a while now, and he told me that the tumor had essentially burst. Cancer is spreading all through my body, and he said it could be a matter of hours or a few weeks. My daughter is going to be an orphan."

How could he turn this down? How could he tell his friend he was willing to do anything for him except that?

"I have you named in the will." Charles's voice trailed off as he coughed. Then, it came back, coarse and tired. "It won't hold up in a court of law. Of course. You're not bound. But I want you to have half custody."

"Me? Wait. Half?"

"Yeah. The other half goes to the woman my wife, Kendra, chose."

"How will I do that?" he asked immediately. How do you have half custody of a child?

"We thought you two could figure it out. I need to go. I want to talk to my daughter before I can't."

Of course. He wouldn't dream of keeping him on the phone. Keeping him from having one last conversation with his child.

"How am I going to—"

"I have it all together. You'll get the information. I just didn't want you to be blindsided. I... You're the most upright man I know. I can't think of anyone else I'd rather have with my daughter. I know you'll do the very best you can. And the same for the woman my wife chose. And I know you'll...get along with her." His voice faded, and then he said, "Oh. There's a horse too."

He might want to get along with her, but if she lived in another state, how were they going to see each other? He couldn't remember the last time he'd driven out of North Dakota. Last time he went to the Cities, which was more than ten years ago.

And a horse? What was that about a horse? Of course, he felt a lot more qualified to handle a horse than he did a little girl.

Still, he said goodbye to his friend, most likely for the last time on this earth, and they hung up.

Part of him urged him to call back and try to talk to Charles again. Convince him that he would be a very terrible father, and part of him thought that he wouldn't actually go through with it. That someone would put a stop to it. A grandparent, or an aunt, or a sister. Someone who would want that little girl and wouldn't allow her to go to a stranger.

Yeah. That's probably what would happen. Someone else would contest the will, and the child would stay in the family where she belonged. He didn't need to worry about it.

Chapter 5

Brooklyn sighed and put her elbows on the desk and her head in her hands. She closed her eyes tight, squeezing them against the irritating dryness from staring at her computer screen.

The numbers didn't lie. Their farm was slowly going under.

Her sisters and she tried hard, selling things at the farmers markets, making baked goods, and growing vegetables.

They had had several setbacks, lost a crop of broccoli that they'd invested heavily in, and Ainsley had been hospitalized with an infection last winter.

Their insurance covered most of it, but not all.

Their savings had been wiped out, and they had been slowly getting behind. They could make things work if they could just catch a break and not have any setbacks for a while, but...it just didn't seem like that was happening.

Her sisters were going to want to talk to her at supper tomorrow. They would be leaving early for the farmers market, while she had to go into town.

They'd want a report. She could probably put it off for a couple of weeks, using the distraction of the farmers market tomorrow, but she was going to have to tell her sisters that if something didn't change, they were going to lose the farm.

Not exactly words she wanted to have to tell them.

For what felt like the millionth time that night, she forced her eyes open, her head back, and looked at the spreadsheet in front of her. There had to be an answer. Just had to be.

But nothing materialized, and she went to bed dejected.

In the morning, she helped her sisters pack the car, answering their questions with noncommittal answers of her own, when she couldn't deflect or change the subject.

Somehow, sometime soon, if she hadn't found an answer to their problems, she would have to find a way to tell them.

In the meantime, she wasn't going to upset their day.

They laughed and joked, and if anyone noticed that she wasn't quite as jovial as she usually was, none of the other girls said anything. It was early, not yet dawn, and maybe they really didn't notice.

Or maybe they suspected, and they didn't want to ruin their day either.

Whatever it was, they laughed and eventually left, and she went back in the house, packing the things they had earmarked to take in to the church rummage sale.

It took longer than she expected. It was after nine when she had packed the last bag and grabbed her purse.

As she had her hand on her doorknob, her phone rang, and she pulled it out, noting that she did not recognize the number.

"Hello?" she said, half expecting it to be a telemarketer.

"Brooklyn Lepley?"

"This is she."

"This is Charles Lessing. You knew my wife."

"Yes. I remember. She was my roommate, and I met you at college. I...was at your wedding." It was one of those times where she had been deliberately, it seemed, paired up with Cormac. She didn't resent it or have bad memories of the wedding. It was just marked in her mind as a "Cormac time."

"Yes. My wife thought very highly of you."

The man's voice sounded much older than the man she remembered from the wedding. Strangely so. But it finally dawned on her that he was talking about Kendra in the past tense.

"Did something happen?" she asked, her words coming out quickly, concern lacing every one of them.

"She passed away in a car accident several years ago. It...broke my heart. Maybe you hadn't heard."

"No. I hadn't. I'm so sorry." She couldn't believe it. She'd gone to school with her. Such a laughing, happy, fun person. She was always telling Brooklyn that she was her anchor. The one who kept her straight. The person she looked up to, which Brooklyn never understood because Kendra was always so sweet and happy, and Brooklyn admired her.

Regardless, her throat closed and her stomach felt empty, full of sour air.

"I'm dying of cancer."

"Oh no." Why was he calling to tell her that? She didn't know what to say. She felt bad, of course, but wasn't sure what she was supposed to do.

"I'm sorry. I didn't call to make you feel bad. I called for something much more urgent."

"More urgent?"

"My wife loved you. She admired you. She always said that she thought you would be a great mother, and if anything ever happened to her...she wanted you to raise our daughter."

"But—"

"I have hours, maybe days. No more. I have the paperwork put together, and it's on its way to you. Please consider. For me. For her. For our daughter."

"Of course. I'll... I'll do it."

"You'll share custody with...someone." He sounded a little confused, like his breathing was labored and he needed to focus on it, and if he was that close to dying, it probably took monumental effort for him to even make a phone call to begin with.

"You rest. Whatever comes, I'll take care of her."

"There is a horse..."

A horse?

Brooklyn almost asked him to repeat himself. What was she going to do with a horse? She didn't know anything about horses. Not much. True, they had a ranch and some beef cattle, but they didn't run anything big. The cattle were enough to pay the mortgage for a couple of months in the winter when the baked goods and vegetables weren't selling.

Then she realized, he'd said she was going to share custody? Forget about the horse. Who was she going to share custody with? Of course, whatever came, she would do it. That's what she said, and she would do her best to keep her word. If it was humanly possible, she would.

Of course, this was about the strangest thing that anyone had ever done to her or that she had ever even heard of. But she remembered Kendra from college, they'd been really good friends, and she couldn't let her friend down. Even if they had drifted apart, and she hadn't even known she passed away.

Caring for her daughter.

What would that be like?

Chapter 6

Several weeks later, it came as no surprise to Cormac that he had a registered letter that he needed to sign for at the post office.

So, once he was done with the ranch chores, he figured he'd go into the diner and have lunch, then pick up his letter once the post office reopened for the afternoon.

He almost changed his mind when he opened the diner door and saw Brooklyn sitting at the counter, chatting with Jane, the owner.

He almost missed her, because he'd seen the sign for cooking classes, which reminded him that he'd thought about taking them.

He'd heard there was a group of old men who took them on Sunday afternoons, and it was quite entertaining. Knowing that, and he was getting tired of the same old same old and figured a few hours of entertainment and a new recipe or two to try might be a good thing in return for an investment on a Sunday afternoon.

Doubly so, if he was going to end up with a child. It wasn't that he couldn't cook. But maybe his meals weren't exactly child friendly. He didn't even know how old the girl was. He hadn't thought to ask.

Not that it mattered. He'd told Charles he would do it, and whatever the age, he would have to keep his word.

Sometimes he wished he wouldn't jump into things with both feet and would take a little bit of time to think about them.

But could he have told his friend no?

He hoped not. He wouldn't want to be that kind of person who wasn't willing to have his life disrupted in order to do someone a favor.

Or who would be scared off by a favor of this magnitude.

It was an honor to be asked to take care of someone's child. He wouldn't take it lightly.

Ignoring Brooklyn, who twisted in her seat to see who walked in, he lifted a hand to Jane and said, "I'll take a burger and fries along with a Coke whenever you get time," and walked over to the corner booth and sat down.

Sometimes he looked at the menu and ordered something a little fancier, but he just wanted to eat, get his letter, and go back home and try to figure out what in the world he was going to do.

Hopefully his letter told him where the woman who was going to share custody of the child lived. Maybe her name. Maybe he was going to share custody with a grandmother.

Maybe, if he were blessed, he would only have her during the summers, and the grandmother or aunt or whoever shared custody with him would have her during the school year.

Not that he didn't want her, just...that would make things easier on him.

Feeling ashamed that he had been more concerned about easy than right, he tried to make his thoughts go in a different direction. Thinking about the crop dusting that he hired and trying to figure out what he could do to increase his income on the ranch.

Jane brought his food out, chatted with him for a bit, and went back behind the counter. He was almost finished eating when the door opened and the bell chimed.

He didn't look up, assuming it was Brooklyn leaving.

He ate the last of his fries, grabbed his garbage, threw it away, and took his plate and cup and utensils to the counter.

He laid enough cash down to cover his meal and give a generous tip.

"It was excellent, as it always is. Thanks, Jane."

"My pleasure," she said.

"What's up with the cooking class on Sundays? Anybody allowed to come?"

"Yep, anyone. And like it says on the sign, it's free. You just let me sell what we make. Although, I usually let students take food home if they want."

"If I do, I'll pay for it. That's not a big deal."

"You're thinking about coming?"

He nodded, not wanting to get into the changes that might be happening in his life.

"I'll see. I thought about it." He nodded at his empty plate. "Thanks again for lunch."

"My pleasure," she said with a grin.

He returned her smile and walked out.

Sweet Water's post office wasn't very big. There was a much bigger rural delivery than there were PO boxes, but it's where people had to come if the mail person couldn't fit their boxes in the car, if they had to sign for letters, and if the mail person missed them.

He almost walked by when he saw Brooklyn's head in the window.

It was a small post office, and he wouldn't be able to go in and get his letter without talking to her. Or at least brushing by her, where it would be obviously rude if he didn't say anything.

He had never gone out of his way to avoid another person, except the few times he'd done it with Brooklyn. He adjusted his hat on his head and straightened. He wasn't going to allow her to dictate when he picked up his mail.

Taking a deep breath, laughing at himself while he did it because seeing one small woman at the post office should not take all the bravery he possessed, he put a hand on the door and walked in.

Brooklyn, chatting with the postmistress, Mrs. Sherry, didn't turn around to look at him.

But after Brooklyn had said thank you and taken her mail, Mrs. Sherry said, "Cormac! I don't think I've ever seen you two in here together before."

That of course made Brooklyn's head jerk up from where she was looking at the mail in her hands.

Her eyes widened, then narrowed and her jaw set.

Cormac braced himself. He would jerk his head in acknowledgment of her presence regardless of what she did. But he wouldn't do more than that. And despite his best intentions, he didn't move over to let her by.

But as he was bracing himself, she seemed to deliberately relax the muscles in her face, and while he wouldn't call it a smile, her lips relaxed so they weren't pressed together.

"Cormac. I... I..." She took a breath, almost as though breathing would help her get words out.

"Whatever insults you're going to hurl at me, save it." He took two strides, brushing by her, but just barely, and forcing her to back up, without exactly shoving her.

It was rude, and he felt like a heel even as he was doing it. Mostly because he saw the look on her face, surprise and a little bit of hurt, like maybe she had been going to say something that wasn't rude, and he had ruined the opportunity.

Why did he have to be like that?

Because she had hurt him, more than once, and he didn't want to allow himself to be vulnerable again.

It would just be best if they managed to avoid each other. He should never have walked in the post office knowing she was there.

"Beautiful day," he said casually as he strode to the counter, ignoring what Mrs. Sherry had said about the two of them being in the post office together.

Sure enough, there was a bit of a breeze as the door opened and he assumed Brooklyn walked out.

He did not, no matter how much he wanted to, turn his head to check.

It didn't take long for him to get his letter. That was all that he was there for, and he walked out holding it.

He didn't really want to open it in town in front of everyone, but he didn't want to wait until he got home. So, holding it down at his side, as casually as he could, he started walking toward his truck.

Noticing Brooklyn sitting on the park bench ahead, he crossed the street to the other side and walked by, keeping his eyes turned toward the buildings on his right, not seeing them but making sure he didn't accidentally look at Brooklyn.

He didn't want to have eye contact, didn't want to accidentally say anything to her, and didn't want to, God forbid, see her attacked by a cow and have to rush to save her.

Actually, at that last thought, he glanced over just to make sure she was okay.

No cows in sight.

She sat with her back to him on the park bench, her head down, like she was depressed or maybe reading some of her mail in her lap.

Regardless, he made it to his pickup, hopped in, and started it before he opened his letter.

His eyes skimmed down the page before he went back to the top and read it more slowly.

Same information both times.

The little girl was coming tomorrow.

She was going to be dropped off at his house by her grandmother, who was too old to keep her and couldn't, since she was living at an assisted care living facility, and the lawyer.

The woman who was sharing custody was supposed to be there at his house at the same time they were dropping the girl off. He kept referring to her as the girl, but the letter said her name was Quinn.

There was some legal mumbo jumbo and some information about guardianship and papers.

He'd sort all that out later. The thing he was most interested in, who he was sharing custody with, wasn't in the letter.

He was going to be a father. This thing was really happening.

That meant Charles must have passed away, and he hadn't even known. The thought made him sad and made him feel his mortality in a way he hadn't before. After all, Charles was the same age as he was, and if he could die...

Shaking that thought off, he skimmed down the letter again, trying to figure out how old she was.

He had missed it the first two times but saw that her age was listed as seven years old.

What grade was a seven-year-old in in school? What were they interested in? What kind of bed did he need to get her? What kind of food did she eat? How was he going to run his ranch and take care of a child? How was he going to get along with whoever he shared custody with?

He wished he would have had her name and contact information so that they could have gotten together before the child came and worked something out, just so they weren't hashing things out in front of Quinn.

Quinn. That was her name. Quinn.

It sounded strange to his ears. But everything sounded strange to him right now.

His palms tingled, and something that felt very much like panic swirled in his chest. He wasn't prepared for this. He couldn't do it.

He might have gone to the Piece Makers at one point, but since Miss Charlene had gotten married, they weren't meeting as regularly in the church.

But Miss April might be at the community center.

Sometimes she had some ladies with her, and while they weren't matchmakers, they were ladies who might have information or advice for him on how to raise a child.

He sat in his truck, facing the community center. Maybe that's why he thought of it, or maybe there was something about Miss April that made him feel safe. Less panicked. Like she wouldn't let him do this on his own.

He wasn't sure exactly where he got that idea, because he wasn't exactly close friends with Miss April or the other two ladies who met with her. What were their names? June and Helen, he thought. He saw them in church but had never really had a whole lot of reason to stand around and talk to them.

Not like he did now.

Tapping his hand on the steering wheel, he considered whether he should go forward with the idea or not.

Would it be terrible if he walked in the community center, just casually striding in and just, you know, asking for some child-raising tips.

Was that too weird?

He berated himself. He was about to become a parent. He was supposed to be weird. That was the main job of being a parent. Being weird.

No. The main job of being a parent was to do his very best for the little girl who was going to be in his care. He couldn't worry about whether or not he was being weird. If he could get some good advice or at least something to give him a lifeline so that he didn't feel like he was drowning in quicksand, he would take it. No matter how odd it made him look.

With that thought in mind, he shut his pickup off, opened the door, and got out.

Chapter 7

Brooklyn stared at the letter in her hands.

It was real. She had pretty much convinced herself that the phone call had been a hoax. But when she got the notice that she had a registered letter at the post office, part of her had realized that maybe it wasn't a joke.

Part of her had thought it was coincidence.

That part had been wrong.

Now, the idea that she was actually going to have custody of the child was sinking in.

She was going to be in charge of a child.

With some kind of mystery man. His name had not been given, which bothered her. After all, she was going to be in charge of a child. Have a child. And she was going to have to somehow get along with the man who was sharing custody with her. Like a divorce, only she didn't even know the man.

This was going to be difficult to explain to her sisters.

To say the least.

She figured she'd sat on the bench long enough that Cormac had left town. She had been going to apologize to him. That's what she said she was going to do the next time she saw him. But he had been too rude, and she had been taken aback. Not by his rudeness, because she expected that from him. It was the idea that someone was watching, and she couldn't even get the words out before he'd been rude to her.

She deserved it though, after the way she treated him last time they were together.

An oink disturbed her concentration. She glanced up, seeing Sweet Water's own pig amble up beside her.

She hadn't been this close to it, although she'd seen it around. She hadn't realized it was friendly. A couple of times when she'd seen it, it had been running from the cow, a Highlander the townspeople called Billy.

She hadn't actually heard of anyone petting it, although she knew several different people who fed it.

It came over, grunting, and pushed her with its nose.

She'd heard that pigs bite, but she kept herself still, not wanting it to know that she was a little bit afraid of it.

Tentatively, she reached out a hand and started scratching around its ears. It grunted in pleasure, which encouraged her, and she scratched a little harder.

It held still, its odd-looking eyes half closed in what looked like ecstasy as she scratched first one ear then the other.

The pig pushed closer and rolled its head from one side to the other, encouraging her to keep scratching.

Despite her problems and everything she'd been thinking, she smiled. Something about animals and how they relaxed a person tumbled through her head.

Wouldn't it be nice to be a pig who wandered around the town where various people fed and took care of you, and you didn't have a care in the world?

Immediately, she knew she wouldn't be happy with that. She wouldn't be happy having everyone do everything else for her and having no purpose of her own. In short, life came with problems. But God didn't give problems without giving a person the ability to go to Him, not just for solutions, but for comfort when they were upset.

Maybe not quite the way the pig had come over to her for a pat on the head, but she could approach God just as boldly. Talk to him about the issues she faced, and He cared for her far more deeply than she could ever care for a pig.

He wanted to help her. Wanted to guide her in the right direction. Wanted to work all the things in her life out for her good and for His glory.

She forgot that sometimes. That life wasn't about her comfort and ease and enjoyment. It was about giving glory to God.

Of course, God wanted her to have comfort and enjoyment and occasional ease, but having it all the time would not be good for her.

An overwhelming sense of gratitude filled her soul. Gratitude for a God who loved her, and would not allow her to skim through life, but gave her trials that challenged her, grew her, and made her into a better person.

The financial issues on the farm, this child that she didn't know, a person to share custody with, her sisters depending on her and wanting her to give them a good report of the farm, all oppressed her. Even the kissing booth.

God was behind it all. He was orchestrating her life in such a way that all things would work out for good.

And with this overwhelming sense of gratitude came an even stronger feeling that she wanted good for herself, true, but she wanted glory for God even more.

Lord, please, whatever these trials are that You're sending into my life, whatever they're for, help me to use them to glorify You and to show others how amazing You are.

That was really her heart's cry. Sometimes she forgot it. Like when she was around Cormac. Sometimes the selfishness in her soul took over, the sinful nature that she was born with wanting dominance over that part of her that longed to worship and love God.

She wanted to remember what she was really here for, and it wasn't for herself. It was for others. So she was going to do the best she could with this child, and when she found whomever she was sharing custody with, she would do her very best to get along with them and be kind and not punish them, on purpose or accidentally, because she had not been expecting this. She would pull her share, more than her share if necessary, and do whatever it took to do the very best for the child.

And the horse. She'd do whatever needed to be done with the horse too, although she really wasn't sure what that was.

Regardless, sitting there, scratching the hog, things became more clear. She needed advice on the child, and she would go see the ladies at the community center, to see what they had to say, and she would try to remember, as best she could, that this was about God and not about her.

She sat back, content with this new direction in her life and hoping that she could remember this when things got chaotic, because things always got chaotic.

Eventually the pig ambled away, and she watched it go, its back swinging back and forth, oddly large atop the narrowed legs and pointy hooves.

The sight made her smile.

Finally, she pushed up from the bench and walked slowly toward the community center. The one place where she knew she could get good advice about the future.

Chapter 8

Cormac pushed open the door to the community center and walked in.

Honest to goodness, he almost turned around and walked right back out.

Of all the crazy things to have happen, having Brooklyn already standing in front of Miss April when he walked in was a nasty trick of the universe.

He halted that thought as soon as it came to him.

He didn't believe in "the universe," nor did he believe in it playing nasty tricks.

He believed in God. And God orchestrated things for his good.

Even if he didn't understand them.

Something nagged at the back of his consciousness. Some nebulous idea that maybe he was running into Brooklyn because God was orchestrating it.

The thought wavered and then evaporated like mist on a morning breeze.

Maybe it settled something in his soul, though, and a little bit of the antagonism that he always felt toward her dissipated.

After all, he'd been rude to her at the post office. Very rude.

And while there was a part of him that felt justified for his rudeness, there was a bigger part of him that felt bad.

Not bad enough to apologize in front of people, but bad enough that...he knew he should.

"Cormac, come on in!" Miss April said, peering around Brooklyn, who had jerked, then whipped her head to look behind her at the mention of his name.

He couldn't help it. He might feel bad, but he still smirked at her.

He was in the process of shoving the letter in his back pocket when he saw her holding a very similar letter in her hand.

It had the green line across the top that said it had been a registered letter, and he remembered that she had been at the post office too.

Miss June, sitting to the right of Miss April, put her things aside. "You seem to have a registered letter as well. Interesting. Today must be the day for them," she said in her easy, calm voice. Miss June seemed to be one of the most levelheaded or maybe emotionally level people that he knew. He couldn't recall ever seeing her upset, not extremely sad, angry, or happy.

She just always seemed very content, never getting anxious, and in some part of his brain, he admired that.

Or maybe leaned into it, feeling like she was the kind of person someone could depend on in an emergency, because she would keep a level head.

Then, what she had said hit him. His fingers tightened around the letter in his hand, crinkling the paper.

He was sharing custody of the child he didn't even know with a nameless person.

Could it really be his archenemy? Okay, maybe that was a little dramatic. Brooklyn was not exactly his *arch*enemy. He didn't hate her. Although, he felt like she probably hated him.

They definitely had history, and he couldn't see them ever being anything more than casual acquaintances, definitely not friends. Enemies would be a better word to use to describe their relationship with each other, far better than friends.

Brooklyn, whose face registered shock at seeing him, continued to stare at him, a small gasp escaping her as her hand, holding her letter, flew to her throat, like she was trying to protect herself.

It bothered him, her look of abject horror. Even if that's the way he felt, it was still insulting for her to look at him and act like he was the absolute worst person in the world for her to get stuck with.

That was why his smirk grew wider.

"God wouldn't do that to me," he said, with what he hoped was a confident tone. Because he was anything but confident. He was very much afraid that God indeed would do that to him, and probably it was exactly what he needed because of the attitude he currently fought.

"No. You mean God wouldn't do that to me." Brooklyn's voice was low, horror-filled, the same way it might be when talking to a friend about a meteor heading right toward them, low and soft and careful, and full of every terrible emotion, knowing the end was imminent.

She made a telling statement.

From her reaction, he deduced that his inference was correct, and she was indeed the person he would be sharing custody with.

Maybe you should try to get along with her.

He hated that voice. Hated what it said. Hated that it was right.

He wanted to throw the letter down, say there wasn't a chance in hell that he would work with her, and walk back out.

Maybe God thinks you're acting like a baby and you need to grow.

Again, the voice was correct. He knew it. But that didn't always mean that his actions fell in line with what he knew he should do.

"Cormac, do you have a letter stating that you are going to be getting custody of a child tomorrow?" Miss April asked, her voice reasonable, calm. He needed the calm. Because his insides were flipping out. The idea of being a father had been scary to begin with. But not only was he going to have to be a father, but now, he was somehow going to have to figure out a way to get along with the one woman whom he had not been able to get along with in his life before.

Grow up.

The voice in his head sounded irritated. Cormac wanted to stick his tongue out at it, but he didn't. The main reason being that he didn't want anyone in the room to have an actual reason to think he was an idiot.

Of course, Brooklyn already had actual reasons to think he was.

"I do." His lips flattened, and he held them together, not wanting to say more. After all, if he was going to be getting along with Brooklyn, he needed to start training his brain to think of her as his friend, not his enemy. He also needed to start training his mouth to stay closed when it didn't want to say something nice. The kindergarten teaching he didn't seem to have yet mastered.

"Did you know that Brooklyn was the person you're sharing custody with?" Miss April asked what seemed like a reasonable question, although he supposed it was possible that they thought he knew.

"No." He said that immediately. It seemed reasonable that they might wonder about that. The idea that they could think he knew all along turned his stomach in a way that felt very uncomfortable.

"I didn't know either," Brooklyn said, almost as though she were trying to defend herself, and he felt, for the first time in his life, a bit of camaraderie with her.

So much of his life had been spent, if not exactly thinking of her as his enemy, thinking of her as someone who didn't like him and who, therefore, he didn't like.

"It was a shock, wasn't it?" he said, his words low, not exactly wobbly, but not said with his usual confidence. After all, he hadn't expected to say them.

"It was. I have no idea how to be a mother."

"I don't know how to be a dad." His eyes narrowed a little, as her words so closely mirrored his. It wasn't that his life was going to be upended, he could handle that. Plenty of times in his life, it had been upended. And it wasn't that he resented the intrusion. He hadn't even thought about that. It was the idea that there was a little girl who needed a dad, and he didn't know if he was up to the task.

He liked that Brooklyn's concerns seemed to be along the same lines. She wasn't complaining that she didn't want to do it or that it was going to inconvenience her.

Her concerns seemed to be for the child, and he admired that.

"Did you get information about a horse?" she asked.

"I didn't. I heard about it, but I didn't understand it."

Her eyes widened a bit, and her shoulders went up. "I didn't either. A horse? Who does that?"

"A child and a horse. It just seems so strange."

"I agree. Our...letters must be very similar."

He nodded, stepping forward, but not quickly. Hesitantly, almost as though he wasn't sure whether this new truce between them was real or not.

But she seemed interested, her eyes going to his hand where he clutched the letter still.

She seemed to wait for him to get there as her hand slowly lowered from her throat.

He was the man, he should lead. Slowly, he held his hand out with the letter in it. Offering it all to her. Envelope and everything, just to be open and aboveboard.

It didn't exactly surprise him when she did the same. She didn't take the letter out of the envelope for him but gave him the entire thing, holding it out to him without reserve.

He eyed it for just a moment before he took it from her and felt his own letter slip from his fingers, which he forced to relax and not clench.

He opened her letter, read it through quickly, then read it through again, slowly.

She finished at the same time he did and looked to him as his eyes raised from the paper.

"I think yours is exactly the same as mine," she said softly. Her voice holding...disbelief maybe?

"That's exactly what I was thinking. I suppose we could compare them side by side, but I think we'll find that they just changed the names."

Without saying anything more, they both held their letters up, his in his right hand, hers in her left as they shifted, to look at the letters held side by side.

Their suspicions were correct. The letters were exactly the same.

Not that that proved anything, other than there weren't two children and two horses that were being given away to people in Sweet Water. It was just Brooklyn and him. His earlier thoughts about God arranging his life to work out for his good, including his interactions with Brooklyn, nudged him a bit, and he almost laughed.

He stopped himself just in time. It wouldn't do for him to laugh and possibly destroy the tenuous truce he and Brooklyn seemed to have going between them.

"It seems to me like you two have some talking to do before tomorrow," Miss April said, startling Cormac. He'd forgotten there was anyone else in the room. He'd been so focused on Brooklyn.

Brooklyn seemed surprised too, as her eyes blinked, and she shook her head a bit, looking over toward the ladies before looking down at the floor. Her eyes finally lifted back to his.

"They're probably right." She said that softly, almost as though offering to extend their truce.

He nodded. "How about you come out to my ranch? We can talk about it there."

"That's not neutral territory," she said immediately.

"Neutral?" He scrunched up his face. "We're not ending World War II, we're talking."

"And I would be more comfortable talking someplace comfortable. Not on your territory."

"My ranch is a comfortable place. It's logical. That's where the little girl is going to be tomorrow. It's just a reasonable suggestion."

She acted like he was trying to gain some kind of advantage over her. "It's not reasonable. I'm going to have to be there tomorrow and be uncomfortable, but I don't have to do that today. We'll go someplace where we're both comfortable."

"Fine. You pick the place."

"My ranch."

"That's not very reasonable. Plus, you have allies there, since your sisters are there."

"Are you intimidated by four women?"

"Yeah."

Snickering from the ladies who were still listening to them talk was small indication that maybe he shouldn't have admitted that. But it was the truth. What man wouldn't be intimidated by four sisters who were as close as Brooklyn was with her sisters? Of course he was intimidated.

Brooklyn snorted like she didn't believe him.

"How about the two of you go to the diner, order some lunch, and talk about it there?" Miss Helen, who had been quiet up until that point, suggested.

"There are too many people at the diner. Eventually this is going to get out, but I don't know that I want an audience while I'm talking about it. This is...parent stuff." He couldn't believe he was saying that in conjunction with himself. "I...couldn't imagine my parents going to town and discussing how they were going to raise me with everyone else there."

"Go to the church. That's private, and there's just something peaceful about it. Something that speaks to your spirit." June's voice was calm, quiet, and a little bit reverent.

Right away, Cormac agreed with her suggestion, but he didn't want to jump on it too quickly, because he didn't want Brooklyn to automatically disagree.

He didn't know what kind of person Brooklyn was, if she typically disagreed with the people around her just because she couldn't stand to agree with anyone.

If that were the case, dealing with her was going to be tricky.

He had never heard anyone say that in particular about her, but that didn't mean it wasn't true.

"That sounds fine to me." Brooklyn looked up at him, uncertainty in her gaze. Like she was waiting for him to knock the suggestion down.

"Sounds good."

"But you want to feed her. After all, she's going to be the mother of your child..."

Cormac's head swiveled to Miss April. She had an innocent look on her face, but he was pretty sure there was some tilting around her lips that showed that she might have been messing with him, at least a little.

"I am not the mother of his child."

"She's going to be my child." His words were spoken low. He meant them. She might not be his biological child, but his friend trusted him to take care of her. Chose him out of all the people that he knew to raise his beloved daughter. He couldn't not put everything he had into it, which would include considering the child to be his.

"She's mine," Brooklyn said, and he got the feeling that she couldn't believe she was saying it, any more than he could.

She wasn't arguing, and she wasn't fighting, she was just making a statement, and while there was a lot of him that wanted to rise up and argue, there was more of him that admitted that she needed to love that child just as much as he did.

"She lost both parents. She's only seven, and she's an orphan. I can't even imagine."

Maybe that was the point where he realized that Brooklyn and he had more in common than he might have at first thought.

She had three sisters, while he just had a brother, but both of them were living without their parents. He knew a little of what her backstory was, but he knew he had more than once felt abandoned and alone.

"Me, either." He almost went on to say that being alone had driven him to seek Jesus, and maybe he wouldn't have done that if he had had a big, loving family.

Although, he'd heard tell that sometimes having a big, loving family made it easier to believe in a big, loving God.

People believed because they experienced it.

But he wasn't going to go into any of that with Brooklyn. They might have called a truce, but she still didn't consider him anything more than a nuisance. Someone she didn't have a choice about working with.

"If you think the church is a good idea, how about let's walk there, maybe we can figure a few things out." He hoped his suggestion was nonthreatening.

It seemed to do the trick, maybe his tone more than his words, because she nodded.

"I was here, because I thought the ladies might have some suggestions for me. I... I'm scared about being a mom."

Her lip pulled back, almost as though she wished she wouldn't have admitted that she was scared. She had admitted vulnerability and weakness, and he understood it wasn't something a person wanted to do in front of someone who didn't want the very best for them.

Maybe it was that small tilt of her lip that made him envision her being insecure, but it gave him the bit of courage that he needed to agree. "That's why I'm here too. I am not equipped to be a dad.

I thought I might be able to learn something from the ladies, get some idea of how I can at least fumble through in the way that will damage her the least."

"Yeah. I'm afraid I'm going to mess her up for the rest of her life. And I don't want to do that. I want her to have every advantage she possibly can. I want to do my very best."

"I don't know whether you've come to the right place or not. I'm sure we can give you advice on child-rearing. Give you thoughts on what you should do, but every child is different." Miss April, unashamedly listening to the conversation, answered both of their statements.

"I think that's why God didn't give us a manual for raising children, as in, step one, do this, step two, do that. Because you can't do that same thing with every child. Since they're not all the same. They're not like...cows or dogs."

"Even cows are different. Humans so much more so," Cormac had to say. From his experience in raising cows, he knew there were cows that were easy to work with and then cows that would give you trouble no matter what you try to do with them, including taking them down to just feed them. They fight you, because that was just their nature. It didn't make a lot of sense, but it was true.

And if that were true, it must be even more so with children. The thought scared him. What were they getting themselves into?

"So what would you say?" Brooklyn asked.

"Well, it's hard to say. For the reasons we just said. But I would suggest you assume that she's going to be uncomfortable and scared being that she's lost both parents, and that she's at a new place, and she doesn't know you guys. So, maybe just give her a chance to get to know you by doing things together. By showing her that both of you are there for her and that she's come to a place where people care about her."

"I think that's an excellent idea. Being together, giving her security. Children long for the security of knowing that they're in a safe place. Something about having two parents who love each other makes a child feel safe. They need that."

"Even if it's an illusion?" Cormac asked. After all, he and Brooklyn were not a couple. They were not married, and they never would be.

Brooklyn nodded, almost as though she were thinking the exact same thing.

"Yes. I think an illusion is better than nothing," Miss April said, nodding thoughtfully.

Cormac nodded along in agreement and glanced over at Brooklyn.

But Brooklyn looked a little suspicious. He glanced back at Miss April, who seemed like a charming and sweet older lady. Harmless.

When he glanced back at Brooklyn, the look was gone, and she nodded slowly.

Whatever that was about, he wasn't sure. Maybe he misread Brooklyn's expression.

Didn't really matter. He didn't have any better ideas, and creating the illusion of a family, at least for a little while to give the child security and a sense of permanence in her new location, without the people who had meant the most to her in her young life, seemed like a good idea to him.

"Is there going to be anyone who knows her bringing her? Or is she going to be dropped off by a stranger?" Miss Helen asked.

"Good question," Miss April said, nodding her head.

"It says there's a grandma who will be dropping her off, but she's too old to raise her." Brooklyn glanced at Cormac. Then she looked back at the ladies. "I got the impression that the grandma would like to have been able to keep her but couldn't. Maybe that's the wrong impression."

"I can see how you would think that. It wasn't anything the letter said, just the way it was worded. Maybe an accident, but I guess we'll see about that tomorrow." Cormac hadn't thought that while he was reading the letter, but once Brooklyn said it, he got the idea that maybe the older lady hadn't wanted to let the little girl go.

An idea, so crazy he dismissed it immediately, pushed into his brain.

He had other things he needed to think about. So, he said, "Anything else?"

"If you'd like, you're welcome to come here and ask us any time. I don't know that we'll be perfect in our answers, but we've all been there, and we'll do the best we can for you." Miss April smiled in a loving and kind way. It made Cormac feel like he wasn't alone in this venture.

Of course, he looked at the woman beside him. He *wasn't* alone in this venture. He was doing it with someone who, up until this point in his life, had been a bit more of an enemy than a friend.

Was there any hope for this poor little girl?

"I'm not in any rush, but I'm sure you have work to do. How about we try to hash out what we're doing tomorrow at least and the kind of front we want to put on. The things we might need to work on so that we at least have a bit of a game plan."

"Sounds good." He nodded at the ladies. "Thanks so much for your advice and for your offer. I'm sure we'll be back. I don't think I've ever stepped into anything that I felt less prepared for in my life."

"Me either. Thank you," Brooklyn echoed his thoughts, and then they turned and walked toward the door.

The church was just across the parking lot, and they both headed in that direction. They kept the door unlocked, and the whole town knew it. It was an open invitation for anyone to go to pray or, apparently, to talk.

Cormac had never made use of the opportunity, but he could feel the draw if he ever did have something major happen in his life, the idea that he could go in and kneel at the altar at any time, day or night, was a reassuring thought. Towns should do it more often. Have a church open for anyone.

"I appreciate you working with me on this," he said as he opened the door and waited for Brooklyn to walk through.

"And I you," she said, her tone holding the insinuation that it wasn't just her who had been unreasonable in the past.

He begged to differ, or maybe not, but his thoughts were muddled a little by the scent that drifted by his nose as she walked past.

If kindness and sunshine and courage were mixed with strawberries and cream with a little bit of honey, he kinda thought it would smell like Brooklyn.

He breathed in again. Distracted. He couldn't remember anything that had smelled that good. Not good, just right. She smelled right in a way he couldn't explain.

But he liked it, and he found himself breathing deeply even as he walked into the church.

A musty scent, with hymnals, a little bit of wood, and maybe some pine left from Christmas, pulled in with the scent of Brooklyn. That courage and sunshine, strawberries and honey scent mixed with the comforting smells of the church he'd gone to all his life.

He'd never caught the scent of a woman who smelled so good.

Now, needing to get along with her, her scent calmed him.

She stepped into the back pew, right by the back door, and he slid in beside her. She gave him plenty of room, and he didn't crowd her, sitting down with his legs tilted toward hers, wrapping his arm over the back of the pew and getting comfortable.

She sat far enough away from him that his hand didn't even come close to touching her. She looked less relaxed, sitting on the edge of the pew, her knees pressed together, her hands clasped tightly in her lap.

"We're going to do this," he found himself saying, wanting to relax her. To reassure her, to let her know that she didn't need to be as scared as she looked.

"I know."

"I'm not going to hurt you."

Her eyes narrowed as her head swiveled over to him, her gaze saying that he already had.

He was taken aback. How could she look at him like that? They hadn't even begun this journey. How could she look at him like she knew he was going to hurt her?

Then he remembered. High school. The cause of their feud. The reason they considered each other enemies rather than friends. Maybe they should talk about that and get that cleared up first?

But he didn't know where to start, and they were on a bit of a time crunch with the child coming tomorrow. Girl. Quinn.

"I promise."

That was all he could do. He couldn't prove anything to her today. Just by his actions, over time. That's what it would take.

That's what her looks said, too, because his promise didn't do anything to reassure her.

That irritated him a little, because he was a man of his word. Always had been. And he didn't like having someone look at him like he couldn't be trusted.

"I'm not sure what to do to reassure you about that, and I'm not used to having to, but I will if you tell me."

She shook her head and moved her head back to the front, her eyes downcast, as though the back of the pew in front of her held some kind of interesting information that garnered all of her attention.

Maybe it was time for them to bury the hatchet, and he felt like he'd offered the first olive branch. Now, it was up to her to take it. He couldn't force her to like him.

Chapter 9

Brooklyn sat with her head down, staring, unseeing, at the pew before her.

Cormac had been as kind as he could possibly be, but she still hadn't gotten over the shock of having him be her...coparent? Is that what they were going to be doing?

It was almost too much. The idea of becoming a mom, and the idea of having Cormac in her life on a regular basis.

She had wanted to storm out of the community center, go somewhere, act like this never happened, but as an adult, she couldn't just walk away from her responsibilities. As much as she might want to.

There was a little girl whose life would be impacted by every decision Brooklyn made from here on out; she couldn't just make them based on herself.

And wasn't it just an hour ago that she had sat on the bench in the park and decided that her life wasn't about her, it was about God's glory?

God hadn't waited around before He decided to test her.

She'd always heard that one day with the Lord was a thousand years. She wanted to tell Him that she would not have minded if He'd have waited a day or two before He decided to see if she really meant what she said.

Still, she stayed.

Cormac was being kind, and she had to find the ability somewhere deep inside to respond to his kindness with kindness of her own. She certainly didn't want to.

"So... Are you going to have her for a certain amount of days, and then I'm going to have her a certain amount of days?" she asked, having no idea how to begin the conversation. And Cormac wasn't saying anything.

That didn't surprise her. He was probably waiting for her to make a suggestion just so he could slap her down.

"Do you think that's best for her?"

"No. I don't. But it's not best for her to have her parents die. It's not best for her to be given shared custody. For people who can't stand each other to share custody and be making decisions for her. That's not best for her." Her voice was low, but the words came out quickly, showing her frustration and displeasure.

She would modulate them in the future.

Be kind.

That was about all the pep talk she could summon up to give herself.

"Okay. I agree. None of that stuff is best for her, but I thought we were on the same page, that from here on out, we would make the decisions that *are* best for her. To the best of our ability." He sighed.

"All right. Let's make those decisions. So...You come live with me, because the best thing for her would be to have both of her parents living under one roof."

"No. The best thing for her would be to have her parents married."

Brooklyn's head jerked up. She yanked it over, facing him, her eyes bright. There was no way. No. Way.

He shrugged, his hands out. "I'm just telling you what's best. You're the one who brought it up. Are you going to argue with that?"

She choked any unkind words back down. No. She wasn't going to argue, because he was right.

She swallowed. That is not the way she meant to open the conversation. In fact, she didn't want the conversation to go in that direction at all. Ever.

"All right. So we've decided what's impossible. Now, let's decide what we can do for her, what would be best."

"So we're going to pick and choose as we decide what's best, or second or third best, because we're going to choose not to do first best?"

"You're making it sound like you want to marry me. We both know that that's not true. You don't want that any more than I do."

"You suggested living together."

"I suggested you moving into the farmhouse, where my sisters live with me. It would hardly be living together, if my sisters are there."

She hadn't really meant to suggest that. She just knew that trying to coparent with someone that she barely talked to, never saw, and didn't want to have anything to do with wasn't going to be best for Quinn.

"I'm sorry. I...had a lot of unpleasant surprises today." She looked up at him. "As you have too," she added quickly, because she didn't want him to feel like she was minimizing how this was affecting him.

"I don't think I hate you quite as much as you hate me."

"I don't think I did to you quite what you had done to me."

"About that—"

"No. Let's focus. Quinn is coming tomorrow, and you and I have to have some kind of semblance of a plan. We don't want to hash this out in front of her. We don't want to foist her upon someone else while we argue after she arrives. So, we'll do it now. You can have her Monday through Thursday, I'll get her Friday through Sunday."

"That's fine, until it's time for me to make hay on a Friday. Or what about your farmers markets? And your baking days? Or whatever it is that you do."

"I'm busy. I work. Even if you don't know what it is, you don't have to be condescending about it."

"I wasn't being condescending. I was just simply saying I didn't know, so I was filling in the blanks with ideas I pulled out of the air."

She had to stop getting offended over everything that he said. That was not good for anyone.

All these things she had to do.

Lord, if You wanted me to grow overnight, maybe You could have told me when I woke up this morning.

She knew that wasn't a fair prayer, that God wasn't asking anything out of her that He didn't ask from other people all the time. She shouldn't be complaining. God was better to her than she ever deserved. She should be grateful and thankful. Hmmm.

This was all an exercise in humility, because she did not want to work with Cormac in any way, but in order to do so, she had to humble herself.

God resists the proud but gives grace to the humble.

"What do you suggest?" she asked, trying not to make her voice sarcastically annoying but sincerely humble. There was a difference. A big difference.

Her heart was still on the sarcasm side.

"I suggest we talk about it and come up with something that both of us agree to."

"Which is what we're doing."

"Right."

"Can I ask you what you'd suggest?"

"Well, I had this crazy idea, but...I'm not sure about it."

"Okay." She tried not to sound too interested. She had just been castigating herself because she wasn't being humble, and now,

Cormac sounded a little uncertain, a bit insecure, and blessedly humble.

"I thought about asking the grandmother if she wanted to stay."

"For a week or two in town?"

"Stay with me."

"Oh."

Brooklyn let that idea settle into her brain. The letter hadn't said how old her grandmother was or even what kind of person she was. It was a dangerous idea to invite someone you didn't know into your home to live there. But if she was delivering the child, and the letter took the pains to say that she was too old to care for her, it stood to reason that the child would be attached to her.

"That's...generous of you." She blew out a breath. "And brave."

He huffed out a laugh. "Yeah. I didn't even want to entertain the idea when it came in my head, but if I'm going to do what's best for...Quinn..." he said the name like it was unfamiliar on his lips, but he wanted to put it out there, to get used to saying it, "then I need to not shove ideas away just because they would inconvenience me."

"Yeah." He was right. And she agreed.

"And I figured if the grandmother was there, it might not be such a bad thing to...have you there too."

Those last words were rushed but like he had to get them out fast, or they would disappear, and he would never say them.

Part of her, a very large part of her, wished he wouldn't have.

Because he was opening up his home to two women he barely knew and one that he hated, all because he knew it was best for Quinn, the little girl they'd never met but were now parents to, and how could she refuse to do the same?

"That's...a big change," she said slowly.

"I know. For me too. But there would be parts of me that could buckle down and, at least for a while until Quinn gets her bearings, do the best thing for her."

"I wouldn't want to tell her it was just temporary. She's already had enough changes in her life, and that might actually make it harder for her, if she knew she was walking into a temporary situation and she would just be bracing herself for us to eventually not be together under one roof anymore."

"I see that. It might make it seem less real, less stable."

"Exactly."

Silence stretched out between them.

"I guess I don't see any reason why it couldn't be permanent," he muttered at last. After taking what felt like forever to think about it.

No wonder it took him so long. She was too surprised to say anything. She didn't look at him, but her hands tightened in her lap, and she wished she had something to keep them occupied. A hammer in each one and a rock to hit would be nice.

A house to tear down. Something to destroy.

She wasn't sure why she was feeling so aggressive, so desperate for an outlet for her frustration, such as it was.

"Permanent?"

"You're friends with Smith and Abrielle. You know they got married with the idea that they both wanted a ranch. If they can get married because of keeping a ranch, would it be so terrible to get married with the idea of providing a stable home for a child? For Quinn?" He sounded like he was a little more comfortable with the name.

She admired him for making sure he used it. For being willing to be uncomfortable, for not waiting until she was in front of his face before he decided that he needed to learn it. He was doing it out of consideration for the little girl. For his daughter.

Of course, her brain was worrying with the idea of the name and being familiar with it, just so she could avoid thinking about what he had just said.

Marriage.

Convenience.

She could do that? Her automatic answer was no, but even while her lips formed the shape to say the word, her throat was closing and her mind was going back to what she had thought about on the bench this morning.

Was she living her life for herself? Or was she doing it for God's glory? If God had given her a little girl to raise, didn't he expect her to do her very best? And it wasn't chance that had given her Cormac as a coparent.

She could see God wanting her to reconcile with him. Of course God wanted her to do that. She had known that for forever, even before she knew they were going to share custody of a child. But...did reconcile mean marry?

"To me, marriage is forever. It's not something you go into lightly," she found herself saying.

"No. I didn't say it lightly."

"Why did you even say it at all?" She lifted her head and looked at him. "You can't stand me. Surely there's going to be some woman that comes along that you're going to want more than you want me. What are you going to do about that?"

"Look away."

He met her eyes, unflinching. It was like he was saying he could decide who he loved, who he was attracted to, who he gave his devotion to, and once he made the decision, he would therefore do it.

She admired that, even as she wasn't quite sure whether she should believe that that was actually the way he was. But was he trying to do his best for the little girl? Quinn. Was he trying to do everything he could since he put his mind to being a parent? Who was she to doubt that was the way he lived his life in total? Being given an assignment by God, whatever that was, then putting his hand to it and doing it with everything he had.

She admired him. Even as she wasn't sure what to think. She wanted to hate him. She didn't like the ideas that she had about him being turned upside down, and he hadn't exactly denied not liking her.

"You don't want to be married to someone you hate."

"I don't think I ever, in my entire life, said that I hated you."

Maybe they'd have to talk about that. Of course, she didn't exactly remember him saying that he hated her. He just said other things.

But she didn't have a lot of time to think about it. She had to make a decision, if they were going to greet Quinn tomorrow presenting a unified front.

"So you're suggesting we get married...today?"

"I don't know. Just an idea." He lifted a shoulder. "Do you have a better idea? I mean, we can be like divorced parents and split things up between the two of us, you get her for so long, like you suggested, and I get her for so long, or every day we switch, or every week, or six months and six months. I don't know. People do it all kinds of ways. I guess I just... If I'm going to be a parent, I'm going to be the best parent I can be, and that means doing whatever is necessary to give my daughter the very best foundation she can have so that she is as prepared to live her life to serve God as she can possibly be. And my friend trusted me. He picked me out of everybody he knew and gave me the most precious thing that he had. I can't take that lightly."

She was amazed. She knew her mouth was hanging open. Knew her eyes were just full of confounding disbelief.

He was right. He was so right.

Her friend had done the same. Had chosen her, had told her husband that Brooklyn was her choice. More than that, she knew it was God. God was allowing this little girl into her life. Not just so that she could do her very best for the little girl, although there was that, but God wanted to shape Brooklyn herself, mold her, turn her into someone who was kind and forgiving, and didn't hold grudges, wasn't proud and hateful, but forgave and was humble.

And wouldn't that be a better person to be a mom for Quinn than someone who held grudges and refused to let things go? Who held onto her pride and made sure that no one else was getting ahead of her or putting her down?

Because wasn't that the root of her issues with Cormac?

He'd embarrassed her, hurt her pride, and so her pride demanded that she be angry with him, hold a grudge, not talk to him. Punish him for what he had done to her.

And yet, that wasn't God's way. That was her flesh.

Marriage. That was a completely different story, but Cormac was right. If she wanted to do the very best for Quinn, she would provide a home with a mom and dad.

"This is so sudden. I...woke up this morning hating you. And pretty much everything that's happened to me since then has been pummeling me with the idea that I have to stop." She didn't expect him to get what she was going to say, but she looked over at him, a little bit of humor in her eyes. "I guess I had fallen in love with my hate, and I didn't want to let it go."

He nodded, the expression on his face showing that he was surprised, and maybe a little impressed, with what she said. "I know what you mean. We get certain things in our head, ideas that we hold onto, even when evidence hits us right in the face and we know what we believe is wrong."

She nodded. That was so true of her. "I guess I'm dumb."

"You're not dumb. I think it's human nature to want to hold onto our beliefs, even when facts that refute what we believe are staring us in the face. Plus, no one wants to admit that they're wrong. I think it's a certain amount of laziness too. We have to completely change the way we see the world sometimes, and it's a lot of work. Emotional work. We don't want to do it."

She nodded slowly, kind of surprised at what he was saying. It was almost like he was...defending her. She liked the way that felt but wasn't sure whether she should or not. After all, she'd viewed him as her enemy for so long, it was hard to think of him as anything else.

"You've made a lot of sense. Not just about that, but about the...marriage. I—"

"Same thing goes for you, the question you asked me. It was a legitimate question. If someone else comes along, and you're stuck with me, what are you going to do? I know that once I say I'm going to do something, I'm not going to change my mind. From knowing you around town, I feel like you're the same. That you're a person of your word. That you give it, and you're not going to take it back, just because you have some tingly feelings for somebody else. But..." He looked away. "Maybe you feel like you're better off with someone else, and I don't want to take that choice from you. So no force here. We'll figure something out. This just seemed like a good idea."

He didn't meet her eyes when he was telling her that she might choose someone else eventually.

She could tell it bothered him. And he wasn't feeling arrogant or secure. Maybe that's what convinced her. Maybe that's what swayed her mind. The idea that she might actually be able to hurt him after all. He always seemed so invincible. Nothing she did had ever seemed to have any effect, and yet what he had done had hurt her so terribly.

"I think you're right. I think that's probably the best thing to do, but I also think it's a good idea for us to think about it. I really don't want to make a decision like this, where I'm completely single with no prospects one day and married the next, without at least giving my sisters a little bit of warning and maybe some input."

"I get it. You live with them. That's just courtesy. I... I don't have to do that. Although, even if we still get married, I was still hoping to invite the grandmother to stay. No matter what kind of person she is. You might have to spend more time with her than I do, and if there's care involved, it might involve both of us as well."

"I understand. Thank you for making sure I knew. We... We would be making decisions like that together in the future, correct?" She felt like that was a reasonable question. They were going to get married, but she would not move into his house and let him continue to make all the decisions. She wanted some say.

"Of course. As my wife, you would certainly make those kinds of decisions with me."

"I understand that the biblical model is the husband is the head of the home, but I never thought that that meant the husband browbeats his wife and bosses her around. That's just if we can't come to an agreement, you get the final say."

He nodded. "I hope that's the way it goes. I don't think anyone's ever told me I browbeat them. Maybe I do."

"That's what some of the rumors around town say."

"Really? What are the rumors around town?" he asked with a grin, almost as though he wanted to lighten the conversation.

"That you're smitten with me and are going to propose marriage any day."

He laughed. "The rumor mill had one up on me, because I had no idea about that this morning when I got out of bed."

"Me, either."

"That wasn't exactly a proposal anyway. I suppose... I suppose there's going to be a point in my life where I wish I would have done it differently. Even now, even though I don't know you very well, I feel like you deserved better. And maybe I let you down."

"No. We have plenty to think about. We're doing what's best for Quinn."

"Yes, but in a marriage, you do what's best for your partner too. Kids, they grow up and they leave, but a marriage covenant is forever. You don't expect children to live with you forever. But you do expect that out of your spouse."

Maybe he was giving her a warning. Maybe he was not threatening her exactly but letting her know that even without a child between them, he was expecting their marriage to last forever. Or maybe he was just doing what he always did and letting her know how he was going to be acting.

"This is all new. But I agree. I... I think that you should treat your spouse like a valuable commodity, one you want to take care of, so that you have them for a lifetime." It wasn't that she even went around thinking about it that much. She supposed she'd learned that from somewhere and just put that practice into words. It was true. A person couldn't expect to keep what she didn't take care of. And she certainly didn't want to add divorce to her list of mistakes.

Of course, the best time to figure out whether or not she was going to have to do that was before she said vows to begin with.

As she looked at the solid cowboy in front of her, she felt like if he said he would do it, she wouldn't have to worry about him cheating, and she really didn't think she'd have to worry about him not taking care of her either. But... She wouldn't mind getting the advice of her friends, wise counsel from someone.

"Can I have a few hours? Can we meet back here later?"

He nodded. "I think that is a smart idea. Both of us probably ought to think about this. If we're going to go through with it, we should make sure we talk to some people who can tell us if we're being too crazy. Of course, it's not every day that you get a letter saying that you're going to be a parent. So, maybe our reactions are a little extreme because we've been shocked."

"Or maybe our reactions are unique because our situation is unique."

"Now who is arguing in favor of marriage?" He grinned at her, and for the first time, she felt a connection with him. It wasn't an unpleasant feeling.

"It sounds like it's me, doesn't it?" Her lips tilted up, maybe despite herself, as she looked at him.

"It sure does."

The teasing was there around his mouth, in the crinkle of his eyes, and she liked that. Liked that she was considering marrying a man who wasn't just strong and capable but also had a sense of humor. Who would defend her. He already had today, even though he certainly had no reason to, and she liked even more that he might even make her laugh.

"All right. So, I don't want to push you, but I know we're pressed for time. Quinn is coming tomorrow."

"That means that we should be back here tonight. The church okay?"

"It is." She wanted to say that she would meet him at his ranch, but it scared her just a little. After all, she was *that close* to agreeing to marry him. She wanted to give herself as much space as possible. And going to his ranch felt just a little bit too much.

Just baby steps. That's what she needed to take right now.

"What time?" she asked.

"Seven?"

She nodded.

"Do you mind giving me your phone number? If anything comes up on the farm today, I'll text you and let you know if we need to change plans. I'll try to make sure that doesn't happen—"

"I know what it's like living on a ranch. And I usually have my sisters to fall back on, but I understand that sometimes things come up. It's okay." She meant that. And could hardly believe she was being so considerate to Cormac, of all people. Maybe, when they met back here tonight, they'd have to talk about what happened so long ago. Part of her was saying that maybe he hadn't done anything on purpose.

Maybe she had jumped to the wrong conclusion. If that was true, she owed him an apology, not the other way around, because she had been unkind. Deliberately so. Maybe his slight had been an accident, or if there was some other explanation for it, she should have found that out before she retaliated. Too late. But it wasn't too late to make things right.

He took a deep breath, blowing it out. Even though the conversation was basically over, he didn't move, and for some strange reason, she didn't either.

She felt like she should be in a hurry to go talk to every person she knew, trying to elicit advice from them that would make what she was about to do make sense. But there was something that drew her to Cormac. Maybe it was the antagonism that she held close to her heart all those years. Maybe it was the feeling she owed him. Or maybe it was something else. Something that she could just look at him and see, feel, more likely.

"Have you ever done anything like this before?" He looked over at her. "I mean, obviously not like this exactly, but something that just seems so...crazy. So out of the ordinary. So nuts that you know everyone is going to tell you you're an idiot, but you just have such a...peace in your soul. Like this just feels like the right thing to do. And it's such a crazy thing you almost feel like it could only be a God thing? Ever?"

He hadn't moved closer, but it felt like he had. Felt like his breath washed over her face, she could see the feelings on his. Peer into his heart. Just a little glimpse, like he opened just a part of himself for her, and she liked what she saw.

"Can't think of anything. I played it safe all my life. In the few times I have done something a little out of the ordinary, I know that they weren't the right things. Because I didn't have the peace you're talking about. In fact, I felt the opposite. Like I was doing something wrong and needed to stop.

"This time, with this, I'm a little scared. I think I'd be nuts if I weren't. But... The things I have been talking to God about lately, it just feels like they were preparing me for exactly what happened today. I can't really explain it any other way, other than to say that I know what you mean about the peace. I feel it too. I feel like the Lord's been working in my life, and this is the exact right step." She lifted a brow at him. "No offense, but it's definitely not a step that I would have chosen on my own. And not a step that I necessarily even want to take right now. But the idea that it's the right step is just almost flashing in neon lights in my brain if that makes sense."

"It does. Because those same lights are flashing in mine. And I can hardly believe it, because I would look at anyone who was doing this and think they're nuts. I saw Abrielle and Smith making this decision over a farm, and I thought they were crazy. And here I am. Doing the exact same thing."

"We'll shock the town."

"We sure will."

Chapter 10

"You're thinking about doing what?" Ainsley said, the flour on her face doing nothing to deter from her shocked and baffled look.

Brooklyn had waited until the bread was rising and she and her sisters were well into the pie making before she mentioned she was thinking about getting married.

"I thought you said getting married, but I know I must have misheard you," Zaylee murmured, holding an apple while she spoke.

They always talked while they worked and were quite used to continuing to work even in the most heated or casual conversations.

But this.

Both of her sisters had stopped what they were doing and stared at her.

"Hey, guys!" Teagan said as she walked in the door.

Teagan had married her childhood best friend, Deuce, and they had moved to Fargo for two years to help Deuce's family in their business.

Teagan had assured them that it was just a temporary situation, but in Brooklyn's experience, temporary often turned into permanent, although not always in the way that one expected.

"Teagan!" Ainsley said, lifting floured hands to show that she would come over and give her a hug but couldn't.

Teagan didn't let that stop her. She'd spent hundreds of hours with her sisters in the kitchen cooking, and she came right over, hugging Ainsley first and then wrapping her arms around Zaylee and Brooklyn as well.

This was not the first time that she had been back since she got married, but since they had been used to seeing her every day, and all of a sudden, she was gone for days on end, it was always a treat when she came back.

Her face was glowing, her eyes sparkling. It was obvious that married life agreed with her.

"All right, I didn't hear what Brooklyn must have said, but I heard that Ainsley is aghast at something, so I assume it must be Brooklyn. You are the one we depend on to always do the reasonable thing. I can't believe that they would think that you would get married. Whatever it was that you said, you need to correct them. They're probably panicking."

Brooklyn took a breath, slow and easy, and wondered exactly how she was going to say this.

The best way was usually the straightforward way.

So she said, "They didn't mishear me."

She crinkled her eyes a little, drawing her brows together and lifting them, almost as though she were bracing for a blow. Although she knew her sisters would never hit her, of course. And they would support her, no matter what she did. Even if they disagreed. Which, most likely they were going to disagree. In a very big way.

"She said married." Teagan looked at their sisters for confirmation.

Ainsley and Zaylee nodded to reinforce what Brooklyn had said.

"That's what she said."

"I am pretty sure she said married. I mean, if she had said buried, it would have been much worse, but married is still pretty bad." Zaylee lifted her shoulder and went back to paring apples.

Brooklyn smiled. That was so like Zaylee, to rationalize her mind that something could be worse, then to just be okay with it.

She wished she could be like that. Just be okay with things. She didn't like it when things didn't work out. Didn't like it when things didn't go her way. She was much more likely to grab life by the horns and try to wrestle it into submission. It wasn't that Zaylee didn't care, it was more that Zaylee was a lot more likely to be submissive to God's will for her life. Whatever that was.

Teagan looked over Zaylee's head at her sister. "We can't just let this happen. You don't even have a boyfriend!"

"I'm going to be a mother." Brooklyn figured she might as well get both stones out in the water, get the waves rolling, so she could handle them together.

"You're pregnant?" Zaylee said, her eyes widening and the tone of her voice saying that was pretty obviously something worse than getting married.

"Oh, my goodness," Ainsley said, forgetting about the flour in her hand and touching it to her chest, her mouth open.

"Someone forced you?" Teagan said, her voice low, threat dripping from every word.

Brooklyn appreciated them. Appreciated that Teagan assumed that wasn't something she had willingly chosen.

But she lifted both hands, realizing that everything had come out all wrong. And she was handling this about as badly as a person possibly could.

"No. No, no." She shook her head, looking at the bowl she had been stirring and letting the spoon rest against the side. "I got a letter in the mail this morning. It was registered, and it said that I would be getting half custody of a little girl. Her name is Quinn." She briefly told them about Kendra from college, her husband, their deaths, and everything.

By the time she was finished, her sisters were nodding as she'd known they would.

"I'm not pregnant. But I am going to be a mother."

"Wow. What a major unexpected thing happening in your life," Ainsley said, and Brooklyn grinned a little at the usually unflappable Ainsley seeming amazed that Brooklyn was handling this with such aplomb.

"I can't believe that someone would expect you to just totally upend your life...and give you a human."

"A child of God. Something God created, someone He loves. Of course I'm going to upend my life for them. Isn't that what life is? People? God? And bringing the two together?"

Things like this boiled life down to its essentials. Because all the things they were doing, things to make a living, things to make their lives better, to improve themselves, those were things that really didn't matter in the long run, if they didn't use them for God. After all, everything that wasn't done for the Lord was going to burn.

"I'm glad she did. I really am." She looked around at her sisters. They were digesting the news, and she gave them time. She knew they would come to grips with everything eventually and rally around her. That's what family was for. But it was a blow to her, shock and surprise, and she couldn't expect them to take any less time than she had to get used to the idea.

"You said co-custody? Is that a new buzzword I'm not familiar with?" Teagan said finally, her voice holding her uncertainty as she went over to the sink and washed her hands.

"I don't know if it's a new buzzword or not, but it means I'm sharing custody with the man they want to be her father."

"And who is that?" Ainsley said, possibly seeing a potential romance in the making. Ha. If only she knew.

Brooklyn took a breath, knowing that her comment was going to elicit emotion. What emotions those would be, she wasn't entirely sure. "Cormac Henderson."

"No!"

"You're kidding!"

"You cannot be serious!"

Yeah. She figured that was pretty much going to be the way it was. And it was all her fault. She had spoken so terribly about Cormac over the years. Had insisted that she would never speak to him, have anything to do with him, that he was a terrible person, and now here she was.

Standing in a hole of her own making.

Lord, You couldn't have orchestrated this any better for me, could You?

She took just a minute to think about how amazing God was and the brilliance of His plan.

For having set up everything to help her become a better person because there was no way she could walk through this with grace, without growing.

"What are you going to do?" Ainsley asked, concern in her voice.

"Are you going to try to get sole custody?" Teagan asked.

"That's who you're marrying, isn't it?" Zaylee said, her tone holding wisdom and assurance.

"You're right," Brooklyn said, thinking there was going to be another explosion.

"Whoa. What?"

"No."

"That can't be right."

Her sisters continued with their protestations until Brooklyn put her hand up.

"This little girl has lost her mom and her dad. She is alone in the world. She has nothing except us. And my friend thought I would do the very best I could for her daughter. She gave me the most important thing in the world to her. And Cormac's friend did the same for him. They picked us out of all the people in the world to raise their daughter together. I... I just can't be more concerned about myself than I can be for Quinn."

"I love the name," Teagan said softly. "And I love what you just said. I don't know that I would have thought of that on my own, but it makes total sense when you're speaking. She needs adults who are going to be adults and think about more than just themselves. And you've risen to the occasion."

"Well, I haven't risen to anything yet. I don't know if this is the best decision, although I feel like there's a peace. I feel like this is actually the right thing to do, as crazy as that sounds."

"And you actually...spoke to Cormac?" Ainsley said, her eyes narrowed, like she couldn't quite believe that the seemingly impossible thing had happened.

"Yeah. We ran into each other at the post office. He wasn't nice. Although before that, we ran into each other on the sidewalk, and I wasn't nice. Then, I decided I would go to the community center and see if I could talk to Miss April and Miss June and Miss Helen because I picked up my letter at the post office and I didn't know what to do. I've never been a mom. The idea of who I was coparenting with wasn't really an issue, until Cormac walked in, having the same idea, and we realized that our coparents were each other."

"So you talked to the ladies together?"

"A little. They said we could come back for parenting advice at any time. I definitely don't feel qualified to be a parent, and I feel like he feels the same, but we went to the church, and we sat down and talked."

"Did he apologize for what he did to you?" Teagan asked, coming over and putting her hands in a bowl that held flour and lard, beginning to mix it together.

"We didn't even talk about that."

"You're going to have to. You can't get married and just pretend it never happened," Zaylee said calmly, continuing to roll out pie dough and fit it into pans.

"I know you're right. And we're meeting again at seven o'clock. I suppose we'll talk about it then, but the first order of business is to figure out how we're going to share custody of Quinn. The marriage thing is still on the table, and we're thinking hard about that."

"Did you suggest that, or did he?" Ainsley asked.

"He did. But as soon as he did, I knew it was the right thing to do." She looked down, stirring a bowl of sugar and cinnamon before she admitted what she had said. "I suggested we live together."

There were gasps.

"Here. With you guys. And Quinn. He could go to his ranch and work and come back here in the evening to be a dad. But he didn't like that idea, and honestly, I don't either. I like what he suggested much better. It's more permanent for Quinn, and also he suggested offering to let the grandma live with us too."

Was she already thinking of herself and Cormac as an "us?"

It appeared so.

"So you might really be getting married?" Ainsley said, sounding sad and a little horrified.

"I'm sorry. I know we're still adjusting to Teagan leaving, but...I wouldn't be leaving us, I would still be working here." This was not the time for her to talk about the ranch and the finances and how they weren't going to be able to continue what they were doing anyway. She had never had that conversation and wasn't going to try to have it now.

Maybe she should recommend they sell. But she figured she had dropped enough bombshells on them already. People could only handle so much at one time, and she'd already given them more than enough to think about. And to wrestle with.

"I haven't talked to Cormac about what it would look like. Obviously, the whole point of this is to do the best for Quinn and...marriage..." She wasn't sure when that word had become so hard to say. "It's the best thing for Quinn. So, a huge chunk of my time would have to be taken over with being a mom. But we still have to make a living as well, and so we'd have to figure things out."

She wasn't going to drop any more bombshells on her sisters.

"So, I know that this is not normal, and I know it's really unexpected, but I told you I have a peace about it. But I wanted to know what you think. I mean, I know the idea of me moving out, that there would just be two, where there used to be four, is hard and is a change we don't want to face. But what do you think?"

This is where she wished she had parents. Where she missed her mom. Missed having someone to confide in. Missed being able to tell someone anything and always have that security that no matter what she said to them, they would love her anyway, because they were her parents and that was their job.

Except, some people's parents didn't do their jobs. Some people's parents left. Of course, some people's parents died, and it wasn't like they had a choice.

But Brooklyn's parents had chosen to leave. Her dad had cheated and left. Then her mom had decided she wanted to be with someone else as well, and she had left.

Brooklyn supposed she still had some resentment, especially toward her dad and for her mom as well. How could she just be more concerned about her own happiness than for the daughters she had and the life they had built together?

She felt like her mom had basically told them she didn't care about them when she left.

Maybe that was why she had such a strong reaction to being given custody of Quinn.

Maybe that was how her friend knew that she would take her. Because Brooklyn had been in college when it had all been going down, and her roommate had heard all of her feelings toward her parents. Her frustrations and how she felt like they had chosen themselves over their children.

"I guess I want to hear more about you and Cormac. I mean, five minutes ago, you couldn't stand him. And now you're going to marry him. That's a little bit of whiplash for me." Ainsley's voice was calm, but there was a little bit of an edge to her words, almost as though she felt betrayed.

"I started the day hating him. Honest to goodness, I had no idea this was going to happen. But we talked about it in the church. Maybe there's just something about talking in church. Or maybe it's just God working in my heart. Because before that, after I had gotten the letter, I was sitting on the bench and I was thinking to myself about taking a child, feeling unqualified and unprepared. But wanting to do my best. And the idea that my life wasn't about myself but about God. And how God worked things out for my good. Not always for my pleasure, but for my good. And taking a child would grow me, stretch me, challenge me in ways that I have never been before. And I determined in my heart that whatever God put in front of me, I was going to do my very best to bring Him glory, because that's what my life is supposed to be."

"That's true," Zaylee said softly.

"And then, it was right after that that I met Cormac in the community center and we went and talked in the church, and he mentioned a marriage of convenience."

"Like Smith and Abrielle," Teagan said.

"Yeah. He mentioned them, and he said if they could do it for a farm, surely we could do it for a child."

"Didn't he acknowledge that there was animosity between you two?" Ainsley said incredulously.

"He did. And we agreed that we needed to talk about it. I guess that's all we really said about it, other than me admitting that I can't let that color what we do. And him saying that his friend was kind enough to trust him enough to leave his most precious possession to him, and there was no way he could let him down. And if that meant getting married, that's what he would do. Then he mentioned about how it was better for a child to have two parents than to be split between two." She lifted her shoulder. "We talked about stability and what was best for Quinn. I guess, when you put other people ahead of yourself, you realize that living for someone else is so much better than living for yourself. And I realized my pride and arrogance was really getting in the way. And considering that I had just told God I was going to do everything in my power to bring glory to Him, it would be rather wrong of me to throw his proposal back in his face and refuse to talk to him."

"The town is going to die," Teagan said dryly.

"We said the same thing," Brooklyn said with a laugh. "Although that's not why we're doing it. I don't even know if we can consider each other friends."

"I would say that you better work on that. You don't want to be married to someone you can't stand." Zaylee wasn't married, but her words were wise.

"I think we both know that, and I think we'll be working on it."

"I agree. If you guys put the past behind you and become friends, it might work. Although, you do realize that marriage involves more than friendship." Teagan lifted her brows, and as the only one among them that was married, maybe she felt like she had to issue that warning.

Brooklyn rolled her eyes. "Teagan, I know what marriage entails."

"Just checking. I think that you could pretend for a little bit, but I'm assuming that you're thinking that marriage is a lifetime commitment? Or are you guys just going to stay together until Quinn is grown?" Ainsley bit her lip.

Brooklyn shook her head right away. "No. I know exactly how that feels, to have your parents stay together for you, and as soon as they think you're an adult," she put "adult" in air quotes, like eighteen was the magic age or something, "that it's perfectly okay for them to not be responsible for taking care of you any longer and to go off and do their own thing. That's not right, and I don't want to do that to Quinn. I want to be the stability that she can depend on for the rest of her life."

Zaylee nodded as she sliced the last apple, and Brooklyn handed her the bowl of sugar and cinnamon to pour over the top of them.

Ainsley had five piecrusts rolled out, and Teagan was almost finished mixing up the piecrust that would be what they would use for the tops of the pies.

Brooklyn went to the counter to check on the bread. It was rising and looked good.

She could hardly stand the silence in the kitchen. Although she knew that it was only fair to give her sisters time to process. After all, she had shocked them.

But she wanted them to be on board with what she was doing. She wanted to hear them say that she wasn't making a huge mistake. She wanted to know that whatever happened, they were behind her. She needed that.

"I can tell you, from my experience, that even though Deuce and I were friends forever, marriage was definitely an adjustment. I had certain expectations, and he didn't live up to those. And he had certain expectations, and I didn't live up to those. We both had things that we prefer, and we realized that our preferences weren't compatible. We definitely both had to make adjustments and learn to give in and give up. At times, I felt like I've been giving in and giving up more. And I know he's still the same. And as long as you have someone who's willing to do that, someone who's willing to make a vow and then give in and give up whatever it takes to keep that vow, I think you'll be okay."

Brooklyn listened, nodding, her hip against the counter, her arms crossed over her chest. "You know, it's funny, but as I was watching Cormac while he was talking to me, I realized that whatever it was that I disliked about him wasn't based on his character. It was based on something I thought he did. And now, I'm not even sure that he actually did what I thought he did, but at any rate, he has integrity and character. I know that. Then as I watched him, I realized that that was really the most important thing. A man who was following God and wanted to do right."

"It's obvious from the way he's acting about Quinn that he wants to do right. That he cares about what he does. Did he complain at all about his life being completely ruined? Or at least changed?"

"He didn't talk about himself at all. Didn't talk about the adjustments that he would have to make or that he wasn't planning on this and didn't like it. That he wished someone else would do it. He didn't even say that he didn't want her. At all. Not once. He had just found out about it, I mean, he was as shocked as I was, so if he was going to complain, surely that would have been when he would have mentioned anything. But he didn't."

"I agree. Sometimes it takes a little while for us to get our footing after we take a hard hit like that. If he was fine, if he wasn't thinking about himself but was just thinking about Quinn, that really bodes well."

"That's what I thought. I realize that people change. He is not the same man he was in high school. So even if I find out that he really did do what I think he did, and did it on purpose, is it really right to hold that against him for the rest of his life? Do I want to pay for the things I did in high school for the rest of mine? Of course not. I want people to look at the person I am today and judge me for that, not for the child I was ten years ago."

"I agree. That's a very mature way of looking at things," Zaylee said, stirring the apples in the bowl.

"I'm impressed." Teagan finished washing the bowl that had held the sugar and cinnamon and put it in the draining board. "That is far more mature than many people ever become. And I'm not even sure I would have thought that way. I... I'm surprised you guys are willing to put your animosity behind you."

"I'm trying. I'm willing to, but sometimes the things I'm willing to do and the things I actually do are two different things."

"I think we all know about that," Zaylee said, which made Brooklyn want to ask her exactly what she meant.

"I guess you won't be complaining when they ask you to be in the kissing booth at the summer festival this year," Teagan said dryly.

"They already asked me," Brooklyn said, but that made her stomach do a flip-flop. Kissing Cormac when he was her enemy was one thing, kissing him when she was trying to actually have a normal relationship with him might be something completely different. She didn't want to mess anything up. She didn't want to be vulnerable or make things move too fast. Maybe they wouldn't be ready for that. Maybe the kissing booth would mess everything up more than it would fix anything.

"I still don't want to do the kissing booth," she said, almost as though to herself.

"Why?" Zaylee asked, as though doing the kissing booth was the most natural thing in the world. And it probably was. If Cormac and she got married, doing the kissing booth with her husband should be natural, but it didn't feel like that.

"I don't know. Maybe things have just changed too much. I... I feel like I'm not sure where our relationship is going, and maybe being in the kissing booth would make it feel like it's doing something that I'm not sure I want it to do, if that makes sense."

"It makes sense. This is a lot of change for one person in one day. Kissing could change everything again, and maybe not in a way that you wanted it to right away. After all, I assume that you'll get married, but you get to know each other before..."

"Yeah. Definitely. That's exactly what I was thinking."

"You better make sure you two are on the same page about that. He might not be thinking in that direction. Men are different." Ainsley, despite the fact that she was not married, sounded like she knew what she was talking about, and Brooklyn had to agree. Men were different. He might not care. In fact, she would bet he didn't.

She didn't need to think badly of him. Maybe she should give him the benefit of the doubt. Maybe he would care. Maybe he would care about that just as much as he cared about Quinn and making her life better. After all, if he was used to thinking about others before he thought about himself, it would stand to reason that he would think about her in that regard as well.

"I guess we'll find out. I'll be sure to talk to him about that tonight." Her voice sounded confident, but inside, she was cringing.

They would have to talk about money. She would have to admit she didn't have any. She couldn't marry him when he didn't know. And money conversations were never comfortable. And then to have a sex conversation on top of it. Boy, maybe she should go take a nap. She definitely didn't feel up to the rest of her day. But she kind of wanted to talk to the ladies at the community center or, at the very least, to Miss Charlene. Maybe she would have some good ideas of what to do. She matched a lot of people together. She had good instincts. Maybe she would know.

But in her heart, Brooklyn knew that if she was confident that this was what God wanted her to do, it shouldn't matter what the rest of the town said to her.

"I just wanted to make sure you guys are behind me. I mean, I knew you would be, but I didn't want you to be shocked with the information from someone else. And if you have any suggestions for me or advice, I'm certainly interested in them. I am way out of my comfort zone, and it doesn't really look like I'm going to be back in it any time soon."

"I say let the past go. No matter what he says happened, you have to make the decision that you're not going to be offended by anything. And then let it go." That came from Ainsley, and that sounded like really great advice. Brooklyn nodded.

"If Cormac is the person you're going to marry, you need to only see the good in him. Don't let anyone talk to you about the bad. See the best. Focus on the good. That's how you want people to treat you anyway. You want them to look at you and see good. So you look at him, and see his good, and maybe you notice his faults, but only in a way where you say okay, I can cover that one. And I have strength where he has weakness, and that makes us a good team."

Zaylee poured apples into a pie shell as she spoke, then she looked up at Brooklyn, who nodded again. If all marriages were like that, there wouldn't be divorce.

"I agree with everything she said. But I guess I have two thoughts. The one is, don't forget that you are an amazing person too. I think it's right to put other people first. I know that you'll be a great mom, and I guess I want you to remember that. You'll be a great mom. You'll be an awesome wife. You care about others, truly care, and you care about God. And that's what makes the difference. I just want you to remember that." Teagan smiled softly, and then her smile grew a little as her cheeks reddened just slightly.

"The other thing I wanted to say is, don't be afraid to be affectionate. I know that growing up, our parents really weren't, and maybe that was part of why Deuce and I stayed friends so long. I was perfectly content with the space between us, and I never even thought of putting my hand on his shoulder, rubbing his back, touching his neck. But I found that human touch is a powerful thing. And between two people who are married, it's a world of communication all its own. Don't be afraid to use it. It's maybe a little of the mystery that the Bible talks about between a man and a maid, and God created that to be beautiful. I know," she put a hand out, "I know that's not something you're going to need today, or tomorrow, or next week even. But just keep it in mind. Some men, maybe most, crave your touch. Crave the touch of their wife, and sometimes we get busy with things and expect them to be adults and take care of themselves, which they do, but don't be too busy to touch him."

Brooklyn swallowed. Teagan's words scared her more than she wanted to admit, but if she felt peace about her decision, then she needed to take them into consideration too.

Chapter 11

Cormac had a ton of work to do on his ranch. He had just arranged to have his crops dusted, but it didn't mean that there wasn't a lot of work for him in preparing for it. And there were always fences to fix, paperwork to take care of, and things he wanted to do to try to expand his grazing and crops.

One man could only do so much, and he just had to chip away at things.

But today, today instead of going home and getting to work like he should, and without really thinking about it, he saddled up his horse and rode in the general direction of Smith and Abrielle's place.

Smith was a good man, a friend, and also someone who had entered a marriage of convenience.

Cormac hadn't really even thought about talking to him about that. Not until he was facing his own similar marriage.

He'd been watching, noticing, and it seemed like Smith and Abrielle were just as much in love as people who had dated for years.

Was that possible?

And if it was, Cormac wanted to know how Smith had done it. After all, he didn't really want to enter into a marriage that was just a loveless union for the sole sake of making a home for a little girl. Even though he felt like that was a good idea, making a home, a permanent one, for Quinn. He felt that was the best idea, of course.

But if she had to live with parents who couldn't stand each other or with parents who just barely got along, it couldn't be good for her either.

It was clear, he knew that for a fact, in the Bible, that the man was the head of the home. The leader. The one who answered to God for the things that happened within the walls of his house.

He took the responsibility of answering to God very, very seriously.

And as the leader and the head, he felt like it was his job that if he wanted to have a relationship with his wife, he needed to work toward that end. And not expect her to... He didn't even know what he expected.

The first thing he was going to have to do would be to talk to her about what happened all those years ago. He didn't do anything, not on purpose. But whether she believed him or not remained to be seen.

Beyond that, he didn't know how to go about developing the kind of relationship where there was affection and love and consideration, maybe passion. He wanted that. He didn't know a man who didn't. But he didn't know how to get it.

Deuce would be a good person to talk to, but his friend had gone to Fargo for a couple of years, and he didn't even bother riding over to his place, figuring he wouldn't be there.

But he had recently gotten married, although his situation was different. Teagan had been his best friend forever, but somehow they figured out that there was more to their friendship.

How? How did you know that a woman could be a friend *and* a lover?

How did you go about figuring out if the woman felt the same? He just didn't know. But he wanted to. Wanted to figure it out, because he didn't typically go into things just figuring he would accept the lowest common denominator.

If it was his responsibility, he was going to do his best. Marriage took two, but the responsibility clearly lay on the man's shoulders.

And he would own up to it.

With those thoughts in his head, the ride to Smith's farm was over before he knew it.

Smith was out, working on building what looked like raised beds.

Good. He'd have something to do with his hands while they talked. Smith wouldn't turn down the help.

But as he got there, he realized that Smith already had help, and just before he dismounted from his horse, the man looked up and he realized it was Deuce.

"Hey there, stranger," Deuce said, straightening up, lifting his hat, and running a hand over his head before he looked back down at the work he'd been doing.

Smith finished drilling a screw, then looked up as well. "Cormac. You came at just the right time. Another set of hands would definitely be welcome."

"You think I came to work?"

"Like I'd let you do anything else if you're hanging around here." Smith laughed. "Of course, my wife might feed us when we're done, so there's that."

Oh. Cormac shifted a bit, wondering what it would be like to say "my wife." Odd words. They felt like square marbles as they tumbled around in his head.

But the same way he'd gotten used to thinking of the little girl as Quinn, he would get used to saying that, if he practiced.

"I work for food, so sounds like we might be in business."

"I don't know, I feel like I've given more than just a meal's worth of work. I think I might need dessert too."

"I feel so bad for Teagan. You are always hungry, man," Smith said, slapping Deuce on the back before he walked over with his hand out. "Glad you took some time to ride over. I heard you're really busy."

"It's that time of year. I just got the boys at Sweet Briar Ranch to agree to dust my crops, so there're going to be some new things happening around the place."

"Funny how life can change pretty fast," Smith said, with a self-effacing grin as he picked his drill back up.

Deuce handed Cormac a measuring tape and explained what they were doing before he said, "Life really can change on a dime. I never for one second thought I'd be married this time last year. Even six months ago."

"Funny you should mention it," Cormac said as he measured out a six-foot-long board and marked it with the permanent marker that Deuce had given him. "Because I wanted to ask about your marriage of convenience, Smith, and I guess I kind of wanted to ask about your relationship too, Deuce, if you don't mind."

He'd almost squirmed as he said that. Men didn't talk about relationships. And he wasn't sure that he even really wanted to. Actually, he didn't. But he needed to. Needed to do it in order for him to be the best husband possible. He was betting the sacrifice would be worth it. He was sure of it, really, he just needed to have conversations that he wasn't always completely comfortable having.

Both men were silent for a bit, and Cormac again tried not to squirm as he took the board he measured over to the saw, set it so the mark hung off the edge of the table, and cut carefully.

When he came back over, he figured that the guys would probably be talking about something else, but to his surprise, Deuce spoke as soon as he came and set his board down and picked up another one.

"Smith and I come about this from completely different angles, because I had a longtime friendship with Teagan, whereas he barely knew Abrielle. But I think we will both agree that communication was essential."

Smith nodded as Deuce talked, as though he were definitely agreeing about that.

"I might say the long-running friendship is paramount. But I don't necessarily think that's true. Because Smith has a great marriage, and he and Abrielle did not have that long friendship time like we did."

"We had shared values. We had shared character. I looked at her and saw someone who was going to do what she said she was going to do. Someone I could trust. I didn't always agree with her, and in fact at first, we didn't even like each other all that much, but she must have looked at me and seen something similar. And then, it was more about showing that I was willing to sacrifice for her and seeing that she was willing to do the same for me."

"You don't dwell on their faults. You have to overlook them. You have to be able to understand the person you married isn't perfect, never will be. I think sometimes women marry men, and they think they're going to change them. Or they think that he's a bad boy, and all of a sudden, he's going to get married to her, and he's going to stop being a bad boy and become good. It just doesn't work that way."

"Being married to a good woman doesn't give a man character."

"No. I do think being married to a good woman brings out the best in a man, makes him even better, but it doesn't change his fundamental character."

"I don't really think men look at women and think that they can change them, but it's probably true for the reverse."

"Probably. I do think women are more likely to respond to what men do than the other way around."

Cormac tilted his head a little at Smith but didn't say anything. That was interesting. He knew that the genders were different, but sometimes he didn't pay attention to the differences. Other than the obvious ones, ones he could see.

"I guess I'm curious as to why you want to know?" Deuce finally said.

Cormac couldn't believe that they hadn't asked that question right away. He would have thought that would have been the first thing out of their mouths.

"That's a good question. I...only have one answer. I'm about to become a father."

Deuce completely stopped brushing the sealer on the boards and looked up. "What?"

"One of my good friends in college passed away, and I'm getting custody of his daughter."

"Hmm." Deuce grinned. "I thought there was something going on that I needed to talk to you about. I was going to say, buddy, you don't need to know about marriage, you need to know about some other things first."

"No. You can spare me those lectures. I'm coparenting. And the woman that I'm coparenting with has agreed that it might be best for us to just get married. It would be a marriage of convenience." He looked at Smith, who jerked his head, giving him an assessing glance.

"There was a learning curve. Like Deuce said, only maybe a little steeper."

"I see."

"I would say, by the time we got married, we both wanted to. Of course, we might not have done it so fast—we had to because of the ranch, but it wasn't like we were two strangers getting married. Aunt April gave us time to think about it. I don't know that anything would have changed if we had gotten married right away, but by the time a week was over, we knew that we could stand each other at least."

"Quinn, the girl I was talking about, is coming tomorrow. I don't think that this woman and I have decided what we're doing, but I know we wanted to have things settled by the time she got there.

It's possible, I might be married tomorrow by this time." He hadn't thought about that too much. Couldn't. The idea was just too jarring.

"You keep saying 'this woman.' It makes me suspicious," Deuce said, lifting his hat and putting one hand on his head, rubbing over it.

"You probably should be. I'm talking about Brooklyn."

"No!" Deuce stopped what he was doing. "Does Teagan know about this?" He had his phone out already, and Cormac assumed he was pulling his texting app up, going to tell his wife immediately that her sister was doing something really crazy.

"I'm guessing that Brooklyn was on her way out to her house to tell her sisters, so if that's where Teagan is, I bet she knows."

"Wow. She is going to die."

"Yeah. It's going to be a surprise to the whole town."

Smith, who hadn't been in Sweet Water as long as the other men, nodded. "The feud between you two is famous. Or infamous."

"Yeah. Thanks. I don't even know what caused it."

"How about you talk to her about it?"

"I'm going to."

"Well, that would be my first bit of advice. You gotta get that straightened out. You don't want to get married with some kind of big misunderstanding between the two of you that is just going to fester and cause problems down the road." Smith rubbed the back of his neck.

"And if you did something to her, you're going to need to apologize and make sure that she is sincerely forgiving you and doesn't hold anything against you. If she does, you really need to get that settled."

"I know. I... I don't think I did anything. I definitely didn't do anything on purpose. I don't even know really what the problem is. I suspect, but it's not anything I did on purpose."

"Well, if that's true, Brooklyn won't have a problem forgiving you. She'll probably be embarrassed that she was so upset about it for so long."

Cormac nodded, paying attention, because Deuce and Teagan had been best friends forever, and Deuce was almost like a brother to Brooklyn. He probably knew her better than any man in the world.

For some reason, that sat a little wrong with Cormac. He wanted to be the man who knew her better than anyone in the world. Even though he knew there was nothing between Brooklyn and Deuce, it bothered him. Interesting. He wouldn't have said he had any kind of possessive feelings toward her at all, but he supposed he was wrong. Because it turned out he did.

"You two don't think I'm crazy? I guess that's my main concern. I felt like I needed to talk to people. Just figure out if what I'm thinking is the craziest thing anyone's ever heard. And then, figure out what to do to make this thing work. Because that's what I want, to be successful at marriage and fatherhood."

"I can't help you with fatherhood, and I haven't been married that long, but I would say the Bible says to treat her like a weaker vessel. I think that means that you don't necessarily treat her like she's inept, but a woman can't handle stress and strain the way a man can. And it's not that you can't tell her hard things, it's just that..."

"She feels cherished if you take care of her. You protect her but don't keep things from her, but you make sure she understands that you know that you are responsible. You want her to know that you care about her and that you care about all of her, not just what she can do for you." Smith gave him a look, and Cormac understood exactly what he was saying.

He knew he was guilty of sometimes not really having a whole lot of compassion, and maybe that was an area where he needed to work.

"I wish I could give you a magic formula. Something that if I said if you do this, your marriage will be a success. If you do this, she'll fall in love with you. If you do this, you'll never have any trouble. But I don't think there is such a thing. I think there are general principles that you follow, and some of them are just general Christian principles that everyone should do. Forgiving, loving, putting others ahead of yourself, not being selfish, being patient and tender. Gentle. My wife definitely likes it when I'm gentle." Smith grinned.

"Got it." He returned the grin, but he knew that there was a lot more wisdom in those words than just the idea that he needed to be gentle with his wife.

"I agree. It's more about just living your life as a Christian, because you kind of want to think you can go home and you can let your hair down, you can treat your family with grunts and rudeness, and be tired if you feel like being tired, and you don't actually have to put any effort into saying thank you and please and being concerned about her feelings or having a conversation with her. And it doesn't work that way. She's more concerned about how you act when you go home than how you do when you're at work. There would be less workplace affairs if that were true."

Cormac couldn't argue with that.

"Probably wouldn't hurt for you to learn how to cook, if you can. Or just do little things to make her happy. I think sometimes we think that the house is her job and the outside is our job, and we don't really think about how we expect her to be a mom to us, cleaning up after us, washing our clothes, doing our dishes, cooking our food. And that's not really the way it's supposed to be. Or at least, she'll definitely appreciate the effort that you put in. I don't think that Brooklyn will expect you to be perfect."

"Adding a kid into the mix is sure to make it a little bit more complicated, so you want to make sure you're pulling your weight on that, too."

"Especially if she's still working in the family business."

"I... We...haven't talked about that, but I assume she's going to. She talked about needing to pay for things."

"You want to get your finances under control as well. Might as well talk about that when you're talking about everything else."

That was not a conversation he wanted to have. He wanted to go into his marriage financially secure, the breadwinner for sure. After all, there were times that he looked at himself and determined his worth based on how much he made. He figured Brooklyn probably wasn't that kind of woman, but he still wanted her to feel like she was getting something, something good. Something worthwhile. He didn't want her to feel like she wasn't going into a financially secure union.

But she wasn't. His ranch was just barely making it. And he wasn't entirely sure that it was ever going to be a huge success. He would never be rich. That he was certain of. Able to provide for a family, he hoped so. But farming was such a toss-up. Some years were great, and others were terrible, and a lot of a person's success depended on the weather, crops and prices, and too many other variables to mention. A person could work hard all their life and never have a successful farm.

Did he really want to bring Brooklyn into something like that?

Although he knew she knew how farming was. She lived on a ranch with her sisters. It couldn't have always been peaches and roses. Otherwise, they wouldn't have a baking business to go along with it.

"Probably, you might not want to hear it, but the biggest thing is communication. You just really need to talk to her. Don't assume that she is going to hate you because you did something stupid. And don't assume she's okay with it just because she seems okay. You need to talk to her, then you really need to listen. I know, that sounds dorky, but it's the truth." Deuce set another board down on

the pile and then looked Cormac straight in the eye. "That would be my best advice."

"I agree. Talk to her. As long as you guys have character and have the same values, you can work pretty much anything out. As long as you're willing to do it."

"I think we're both willing. And you guys made me feel a lot better. I already had a peace in my heart that this is what we're supposed to do, but you know how you know you're supposed to do it, but you just don't know if you can?"

"And you know how in the Bible there were men who were just the same as you. Take Gideon. He fought an army so vast it couldn't be numbered, and there he was with his three hundred men. I would have been thinking there was no way this was going to work out, but if God really is enough, it's going to work. You just have to do your part."

"Maybe that's what I'm afraid of. If I will be able to do my part."

"The spirit of fear isn't what God gives us. So, if you know this is the direction you're supposed to go, just start walking, do your best." Deuce slapped him on the back, and Cormac figured that his good friend was right. He knew this was what he was supposed to do, and so he would just start walking and do his best.

Chapter 12

June sat in the cold doctor's office.

Why did they always keep these rooms so cold?

She hadn't had to take her clothes off, thankfully, but still, anytime she sat still, she always felt chilled, and this was no different. Worse, because she was also nervous.

She had been supposed to get results from some tests back, but the doctor hadn't given them to her, instead he had called her into his office.

She figured that didn't bode well.

Her husband had told her he would come. She suspected it wasn't going to be an easy appointment, and she wanted to have someone beside her. Someone who would support her and help her in case the news was bleak.

She would have called one of her friends and had them go with her, if she had known that her husband wasn't going to make it.

She even reminded him this morning before he went to work, that she had a doctor's appointment at two o'clock, and he said he would be home in time to take her.

At 1:40, she had called him, knowing it took thirty minutes to get to the doctor's but unwilling to leave without him.

He hadn't answered but had sent a text back saying that he was on the phone with the contractor, then he asked what she wanted.

At that point, she realized despite her reminder and his promise, he had forgotten.

She hadn't answered his text but had grabbed her purse and left.

She showed up ten minutes late and had sat for forty-five minutes in the waiting room before they called her back. Now she was waiting again.

Her stomach cramped, and she held her fingers laced together tightly in her lap.

She tried to breathe deeply and convince herself that bad news wasn't that bad. She would get through it. Whatever it was, she would be fine.

God didn't always do what she wanted Him to do. Sometimes He gave her hard things, and that made her feel like maybe she couldn't trust Him after all.

That was why she was scared. God might be going to allow her to have a hard diagnosis, and she didn't want to die.

The florescent lights felt harsh and hurtful, the floor hard and cold.

If she were decorating doctor's offices, she would fill them with flowers and warm colors and happy pictures and soft curtains and big windows with beautiful views.

She would make them so that they were the exact opposite as the scary words that were surely spoken in them.

She heard rattling outside the door and assumed it was the doctor coming and pulling her chart out to see who she was and what they needed to say.

At that moment, she thought of the doctor, looking at the words, words which were almost assuredly not good, and having to come in here and change someone's life with a sentence.

That could not be fun. Who would want a job like that?

Surely when they had big dreams as a young person, dreams of being a doctor, they didn't think about telling people they were going to die. They thought about saving lives, about making people smile, about healing and helping and contributing in a positive way to society.

Today couldn't be a good day for the doctor either.

The doorknob turned and clicked, and June tried to steel herself, looking up with a smile. She would think of the doctor. Not herself. If this was going to be a hard diagnosis, she wasn't the only person in the room who was going to be affected by it.

She could tell immediately as she looked into Dr. Stewart's eyes, her doctor for the last twenty years, since she had left her pediatrician and found a family doctor, that the news was bad.

"Hello, June," Dr. Stewart said, his voice sounding less professional than it normally did and more compassionate. "How have you been?"

"I've been just fine, Dr. Stewart. I hope you're having a good day."

"I've had better," Dr. Stewart said, then he seemed to shake himself. "We're here to talk about you."

"My test results," she supplied when he didn't say anything more.

He nodded, his eyes holding concern, and compassion, as he hesitated yet again.

"It's okay. Whatever you say, I'm going to be okay with it."

"The biopsy was positive. You have cancer."

She felt the shock go through her at his words. Even though she was expecting it, she still felt like she was going to fall out of her chair.

"Do you need me to get you a drink?" the doctor asked, his hand coming out to touch her shoulder.

She forced her lips up, forced her eyes to look into his, forced her brain to think about what he must be feeling right now. He had just delivered devastating news. Would he go home and talk to his wife about it? Was it something that happened to him so many times they didn't even talk about it anymore? Was it something that he lay in bed dreading? Did it make his days as a doctor harder?

"No thank you. I was thinking those were going to be the words that you were going to say, and I thought I was prepared. I... I hate you had to give me that diagnosis."

Dr. Stewart looked surprised, like not too many people considered him after they had had those words spoken to them.

For a moment, he wasn't a doctor. He was just a man. He shook his head. "It sucks. It's the worst part of my job."

She hadn't expected him to be quite that honest, but she was glad he was. It made him more relatable.

"But you've made it a lot better today. This is a diagnosis that you can handle."

"I know it is. Well, actually, I can't handle it, but God can. And I've been holding on tight to Him for a lot of things and for a lot of years. I suppose this will just be one more."

"Well, you have a lot of treatment options, and I want to go over those with you. If you're okay with that right now. If you think you'd rather wait, because sometimes when we get a little shock or jolt, it's hard to think. Then we don't remember anything that anybody says to us after that."

"No. I'm ready."

The words were true, but as she listened to the different options that he laid out, she wondered, why? Why was it her that had cancer? How did some people have a happy marriage, great kids, financial stability, and health.

And she, her marriage that was far from happy, with her husband who worked all the time. He made plenty of money for them to be financially stable, except he spent it all too, so they were always wondering how they were going to have their bills paid. And while she couldn't complain about her children, not much anyway, she also had this new health issue. It just didn't seem fair. Like God was picking on her. And she didn't feel His love as much as she felt His condemnation.

Did I do something wrong, Lord? Is this some kind of punishment? Are You trying to chastise me?

She knew the Bible said that children whom the father loved He also chastened. And she knew there were times in her life she hadn't done the right thing, and she had needed God to pull her back.

But she also knew that there were decades where she had tried to be the best wife she could be, and it hadn't seemed to make any difference to her husband, who considered her so unimportant that he didn't bother to remember her appointment today, although if it had been the first time he had forgotten anything, she would certainly forgive him. Even though it was rather important.

But that was the way he treated her. She was welcome to do whatever she wanted to do, as long as she didn't want him to do it with her. She didn't really have a husband. She had to find a friend with her friends, a companion with someone else. He wasn't interested in spending time with her. It stunk.

"All these options are open to you, but that was the one I feel you would be best suited to choose. I've seen the best success right there, and I feel that if everything goes well, you have a really great chance of beating this thing."

"What are my odds, Doctor?"

He sighed. "About one in five people with your diagnosis and your particular type of cancer, at this stage, are still alive five years from being diagnosed."

"I have a twenty percent chance of survival?"

"You have a much better chance of surviving next year. The problem is, this kind of cancer often comes back. I'm not gonna lie to you about it."

"I wouldn't want you to. That's fine. So the first order of business is beating it once, then the next order of business is making sure that I don't have to fight it a second time."

"You broke it down pretty good. And a positive attitude is probably the most important aspect of your treatment. If you can continue feeling like you're going to beat it, you almost certainly will. I can't guarantee that, of course, but there is a mind element that a lot of doctors don't admit to. There's prayer as well." He smiled.

She didn't know whether he was a believer or not. Their time together, even though it had been spread over twenty years, had never been more than a few minutes at a time. This was the longest she ever talked to him at once.

"Thank you. I appreciate knowing. I'll take careful pains to make sure that I pay as much attention to my attitude as I do about anything else."

He nodded, then asked if she had any questions.

Just a couple minutes later and he walked out of the room, leaving her alone to gather up her things and to follow him down the hall to pay her co-pay.

Alone.

Cancer.

She could defeat it. Or not. She was pretty much okay with either option, although she definitely wanted option A.

But her marriage? The idea of going through this by herself was scary.

But maybe God had given her a marriage where she was alone most of the time so that she would depend more fully on God.

There had to be a reason. Even though she would really like to have a husband to lean on right now.

Chapter 13

I'm sorry, I can't make it to the church tonight.

Brooklyn hit send and then stared at her phone for just a moment before she went back to packing the baked goods in her car.

Less than fifteen seconds later, her phone rang.

Cormac.

She wasn't expecting that. She figured he'd just accept that it was okay and let it go at that.

So the call surprised her.

Walking slowly back to the house to get the last box of baked goods, she swiped and answered.

"Hello?"

"Brooklyn. What's up?"

He sounded concerned. That surprised her as well. He kept catching her off balance. She wasn't expecting him to be a kind or considerate person, yet he kept showing her that he was.

"I'm sorry. I know we had plans to hash everything out tonight, and I really wanted to. It's best for Quinn. But we had a huge order come in today—someone else canceled the baked goods delivery at a grocery store in Rockerton, and...we need the money." There. Hopefully if she left a few hints like that, he wouldn't be totally surprised when they finally had the money conversation. The one they needed to have before she could allow him to marry her.

He needed to know how things stood.

He didn't seem shocked or upset when he replied, "That's fine. I'll drive you there. How soon are you leaving?"

"As soon as I get the car packed. Probably five minutes."

"That's not enough time for me to make it over. Can we meet somewhere?"

He wasn't taking no for an answer. Not that she'd even really try to tell him no, she just hadn't answered him.

She had to admit that there was a part of her, a soft and tender part of her, that appreciated the fact that he wanted to be with her anyway.

A more realistic part of her said that he cared about Quinn and wanted to have the conversation, even if it didn't work for her.

She wanted to listen to the first voice. Wanted to believe that Cormac cared for her. As silly as it seemed.

There was probably just something in her woman's heart that wanted to be appreciated and cherished.

Especially by the man she was going to marry. She wanted him to care. So her heart was trying to get her to believe that he did.

He suggested a place halfway between their two houses, and she came back with a spot that worked better for the direction she was going, which was north.

He agreed, and in fifteen minutes, they were going to meet.

Her sisters, frantically baking in the kitchen since they had sold all of the baked goods they had planned to take to the farmers market the next day to the grocery store that needed them tonight, were in the kitchen as she stepped in.

"This is the last box," she announced, like they didn't know that.

"I'm sorry you have to go by yourself. It's a three-hour drive. Are... Are you sure you'll be okay?" Zaylee bit her lip.

They could have called Teagan. She had left earlier, before they'd gotten the call, to stay at Deuce's farm. They were going back early the next morning, but Teagan would be happy to either ride along with Brooklyn or help the girls bake.

She might have even offered for her and Deuce to take the baked goods themselves, allowing Brooklyn to stay home.

But they didn't want to bother her. She had enough problems and things to think about, and they didn't want to add to her burden.

Plus, from their understanding Deuce worked pretty hard when they were in Fargo, and this trip was a break for them to get to spend some time together.

Regardless, they should be able to handle everything, the key being that Brooklyn would drive by herself.

"I'll be back by midnight." She hesitated. "When I canceled my meeting with Cormac, he offered to come with me. So I'm meeting him."

Both Zaylee and Ainsley whipped their heads up at her words. Both of them looked surprised, but then Ainsley grinned.

"He offered?"

"He wants to get things settled with Quinn."

"Or maybe he doesn't want to see you driving alone at night by yourself." Ainsley's words were a little sly, and there was less hope and more observation in them.

Maybe Brooklyn had been a little harsh in her judgment on him. Maybe he really did care.

That was hard to believe, since they'd only spent one day together.

Just, maybe he wasn't the ogre that she'd always made him out to be.

Of course he wasn't. She wouldn't even be considering marrying him if she truly believed he was a jerk.

Not even for Quinn. It would be worse for Quinn for her to be stuck with a man who was an ogre than for her to not have a family.

"I know how you've always felt about him," Zaylee said. "But I'm kind of excited about this, because I think he might actually be a decent man. I've always thought that, even though I couldn't argue with you."

"Thanks," Brooklyn said, with not a little bit of sarcasm.

"But I do feel better that you're riding with him," Zaylee added.

"It'll make it easier to stay awake, I'm sure. If I'm angry, I won't be in any danger of closing my eyes and taking a nap." Brooklyn's words were dry, but honestly she was happy to have company on the trip. She didn't usually have trouble falling asleep anywhere, but she didn't typically drive around at all hours of the night either.

In all fairness, her sisters would almost assuredly still be baking when she got home. The grocery store had wanted everything they had, which had taken them all day to make.

After baking all day, they were all exhausted, but this was twice as much income as they were planning on, and there was no way they were going to turn it down.

They needed everything they could get.

The other girls didn't know how dire the situation was, but they did know that funds were low.

Ten minutes later, she was pulling into the spot where Cormac had suggested they meet. He was already there and waiting for her.

He came around to the driver side, and she had a little argument with herself as to whether or not she should allow him to drive.

He had said he wanted to, and while she had heard his comment, it hadn't registered until just then that he expected her to sit in the passenger seat of her own car.

Was she going to do that?

She didn't want him to think that he could walk all over her, but on the other hand, she loved the idea that he wanted to take care of her. She didn't want to ruin his tender feelings and make him feel like she wasn't interested in his leadership or protection.

She supposed, it would be nice if he would ask, but at the same time, she could appreciate a man who was decisive and not afraid to make a decision with confidence.

With those thoughts, she decided this was not the hill she was going to die on and opened her door as he came around.

She stood. "Are you sure you want to drive?" she asked, deciding that it would be okay for her to show that she was allowing him to do it rather than him thinking he decided it so it was done.

"I prefer it, actually. But if you have an issue with it, I'm happy to ride in the passenger seat."

"I don't have an issue with it. I guess... I guess there was a part of me that didn't want you to boss me around and just decide that you were going to drive."

He grinned a little, as though admitting that he had been a little bossy.

"But I guess there's a bigger part of me that appreciates the fact that you seem to want to take care of me."

He paused for just a moment as he was walking by her to get in the car. "Thanks for saying that. I didn't mean it as a commanding 'I'm in charge and you're just a little person who has to obey my every whim.' I really did mean it that I would drive because I wanted to do that for you."

She nodded, figuring as much. But it was so easy to take offense because she'd been told all her life that she shouldn't allow men to boss her around.

"Thank you," she said and then walked around her car.

She wasn't expecting him to follow her around and open her door.

He grinned sheepishly when she looked up in surprise when his hand grabbed the latch before hers.

She hadn't heard him come around.

"I'm sorry. I'm a little slow at this, because I'm not used to it, but seems like the polite thing to do is open your door."

His words were the right words, but he seemed a little insecure, like he'd already pushed into the driving position, and she might really take offense at him opening her door.

She certainly wasn't going to do that. She appreciated what that said. Again, that he cared about her, not that he was trying to subject her to his manly whims. Or whatever it was that some ladies got upset about.

"I guess sometimes I struggle with this, but we can assume the best of people, or we can assume the worst of them. I try, although I don't always succeed, to assume the best. And I figured that you just wanted to take care of me."

He grinned, like her words made him happy, and she was glad she had taken the time to say them.

She'd always figured it was better to talk things out than it was to get upset and jump to conclusions.

Except for Cormac. She had gotten upset and jumped to conclusions back in high school, and she'd never taken the time to try to talk it out.

She figured she was so enamored with her hatred toward him, it gave her the drama in her life that she seemed to crave. Someone she loved to hate.

All on her. Because after knowing Cormac just a day, she finally suspected that she was going to be the one who would end up apologizing tonight.

She knew they needed to get things settled with Quinn, but she wanted to figure out exactly what happened all those years ago. It was about time. She should have done it a long time ago.

So, he was barely back in the car, putting it in drive and pulling out on the highway, before she said, "Back in high school, when we were in the play together."

She couldn't even remember the name of the play, but she had a minor part, and so did Cormac. They were supposed to be a couple who was kissing in the background.

They didn't even really have to kiss, he just was supposed to lean his head down in front of hers so the audience couldn't actually see their faces.

The lead characters were doing something, and they were just background drama. Nothing important.

She hesitated, not really wanting to expose herself. To let him know exactly what he'd done that had hurt her so terribly. She'd been teased, and made fun of, and had spent more than one evening crying into her pillow at home.

She toughed it out at school, retaliating, which hadn't helped anything. If anything, it made it worse.

"Go on," he urged, when she didn't say anything more.

She took a breath. She was just going to put it out there. No matter how stupid she felt. Or scared, or vulnerable. If they were going to make this work with Quinn, if they were really going to have a marriage of convenience, she couldn't not be forthright and honest with him. If he reacted badly to this, she'd have time to not go through with the marriage. After all, this was probably a good litmus test of how he was going to treat her feelings for the rest of their lives.

"You went around telling everyone I was a terrible kisser and that my breath stunk. People made fun of me and laughed at me, and of course, for the rest of the time I was in high school, no one wanted to date me."

Though it had been so much more. Walking down the halls, people had catcalled and girls had laughed at her in gym class, people had walked by her holding their noses at the perceived stinky breath that she had. At seventeen, it had been about the worst thing in the world that she ever thought could happen to her, and she had wanted to run away, just leave school and get away from everything.

"I... I know you're probably not going to believe me, but I never said that." He paused. "Not to anyone. I didn't think that at all. If anything... I thought the opposite. You have a scent about you. Not your breath." He looked over at her, his eyes holding a bit of humor but his expression dead serious. "It's one that I love. One that smells better to me than anything I've ever smelled before. I can't quite put my finger on exactly what it is, it's not your shampoo, and it's not any kind of perfume."

"I don't wear perfume. I don't even own any," she said, when he paused. She didn't know whether he was saying that on purpose, or whether it was actually true.

"No, I think it's just you. It's the way you smell that just is amazing to me. I found myself walking behind you earlier today, breathing in through my nose because it smelled so good." He shook his head like he was being an idiot, and she almost wished he would have kept on going. He was making her begin to believe him. It was pretty amazing to her that he liked her that much.

His words soothed over some of the hurt from long ago. Although he was right, he had no proof.

"I heard the things that happened at school, the things people were saying. The more I tried to argue with people, the worse it got. People teased you even more when I awkwardly tried to say that your breath didn't stink. That I didn't know what kind of kisser you were. I guess that's just the way kids are, so I shut my mouth and figured things would die down eventually." He breathed out. "I never thought you thought those rumors came from me. You know we never kissed. Why would I say we did?"

"To hurt me?" she said softly.

"I liked you. I didn't want to hurt you."

And she realized that was why it had bothered her so much. Because she had liked him too. She'd really liked him. He'd been the same exact man of character he was now, just younger and slightly more immature.

"So that was why you snubbed me when I asked you out?"

"Yes."

He'd come over to her table of friends and asked her in front of them. And she'd turned her back on him, putting her nose in the air and not even deigning to answer him.

"And why you wouldn't talk to me when we were put together as lab partners?"

She nodded, and her gaze was softer this time.

The rumors had died down by the time they were paired up in biology. But it hadn't mattered. The pain still throbbed every time she saw him. She hadn't wanted to have anything to do with him.

"I asked you out because...I liked you."

"I liked you too. I suppose that's why the rumors hurt me so bad. Because...I really did like you."

"Interesting. So we actually liked each other. And it took us years to figure that out. I'm not sure if we should really be pairing up together, since we both seem to be a little slow on the draw there."

She laughed a little, amazed that she even could. Amazed that a conversation that lasted less than ten minutes could dispel years of her thinking he was wicked and evil and mean and a nasty and terrible person. Years of her hating him. Or at least telling herself she hated him, because...she really didn't.

"I'm sorry. I'm sorry I snubbed you. I'm sorry I didn't talk to you about the rumors. They were so hurtful and so blatantly mean, I guess I just focused on myself and how they made me feel."

"I'm sorry. I guess we ran in different circles, and I heard a few times people saying things like that, and I said something, and it just made it worse, but I didn't realize it had affected you so much. Or that it was so rampant around you. Honestly, if I would have known, I would have tried harder to quell the rumors."

"It made that year of school really miserable. But I can see how you would never know. You weren't around when people were making fun of me. And if you hadn't said anything, you would have no reason to think that I assumed everything came from you."

"Yeah. But I guess I should have dug into it a little more, but it seems so ridiculously dumb. I thought everyone knew we weren't really kissing. I mean, come on, I was just standing there with my back to the audience, my face in front of yours. No one even considered having us kiss."

"I know. But I guess teenagers are notorious for being unkind."

"Always piling on someone when they're down. It's like a pack of hyenas."

"Yeah. That's really how I felt. Beaten down and picked apart."

He reached over, his hand settling down on top of hers which lay on her leg

It startled her at first, and she almost yanked her hand back. Not because she didn't want to touch him, but because it surprised her. She wasn't used to having someone hold her hand.

That was only a second or two. After that, she relaxed and was tempted to turn her hand around and thread their fingers together.

But she didn't know whether he was putting his hand on hers as comfort, apology for what happened years ago, or because he wanted to. Wanted to touch her.

She was hoping that last was the one, but she didn't want to be presumptuous. There was a lot of pain associated with him in her past, and while she didn't blame him for it anymore, she didn't want to step out of her comfort zone quite so quickly.

Then she almost laughed to herself. Talking had cleared up a lot of years' worth of misunderstanding, why didn't she just ask him?

So she did.

"Why did you put your hand there?" she asked softly.

The road was almost deserted, the night dark. Nothing but their headlights and the lines on the road going by. It felt like they were in their own little world, and maybe that made it easier to ask a question that she normally might not have.

"Because I want to touch you. Is that terrible?"

But it didn't answer her most pressing question. "Why?"

He swallowed, loud in the silence of the car, and his hand moved a little over top of hers. "I know we don't have the best history. I know, now that I've talked to you, that I could have done things differently, and maybe the crush that I'd had on you in high school would have turned into something more, and we could have a whole pack of kids behind us in the car as we're driving together tonight, but that's not the way things worked out. But we're together now, and the crush that I had on you and the feelings I had then, I'm still feeling. You're still the girl that's always caught my eye." He grinned a little and looked across the seat. "And my nose?" He lifted his brows like he wasn't sure whether he was able to joke about that or not.

She laughed. "Wow. Not sure anyone's ever said anything so nice to me. I caught your nose."

"You missed all the rest of everything else I said? And that's what you're going to focus on? I'm giving you my nose?"

"Thank you. I... I already admitted that what everyone said wouldn't have hurt so much if I hadn't liked you so much. I can see that you're the same person today, better in a lot of ways than the one you were in high school, and you're still attractive to me."

There. That was honesty. More honest than she'd been with herself in a long time. At least regarding Cormac.

"Everyone I talked to says the town is going to go crazy when they hear about us."

"I think they're going to say they knew it all along. After all, I forget who it was that told me that people were always trying to put us together because they think we belong together."

He didn't say anything, and they rode in silence for a while. She wasn't sure where that left them in their relationship. Maybe they were friends. Apparently friends who touch each other, as his hand stayed on her leg, over her hand, and she didn't move it and neither did he.

After a while, with the thoughts of their relationship twirling around in her head, she realized that it might be a good idea for them to talk about Quinn. She hadn't exactly forgotten about Quinn, but the idea that they needed to have a relationship of some sort, something where they weren't enemies, at least, was paramount. After all, they couldn't effectively coparent if they couldn't talk to each other.

She felt like that hurdle had been scaled. If they hadn't exactly figured out what they were to each other, they at least figured out that they didn't hate each other.

So now it was time to think about Quinn.

Chapter 14

Cormac clicked the high-beam headlights down, waiting for the lone car on the highway to pass before he put them back up.

Brooklyn had kept her hand underneath his, and he hadn't moved his hand from over top of hers.

He wished she would have turned her hand around and clasped their fingers together, but he figured just the fact that she was allowing him to touch her showed they had made progress in their relationship.

He hadn't realized how much her rejection had affected him years ago.

He had never been rebuffed quite so publicly. It stung. Especially since he had never asked someone he cared about quite so much out.

It frustrated him in a way. They could have been together since high school. They could have a family right now. They could... He didn't know. Maybe they would have broken up. Maybe they would have had a real disagreement that would have separated them, and then this opportunity would never have presented itself. Maybe their friends wouldn't have wanted them to take Quinn if they already had a family of their own.

Quinn might be going somewhere else, instead of coming home with them.

He didn't know what would have happened, and the real idea remained that maybe he just needed those years to grow up. He definitely was a different man now than he was all those years ago, more mature, a stronger Christian, more patient and less selfish. At least he hoped all that was true.

Whatever it was, he knew God was in control. If they had been meant to be together, all the teasing and rebuffing in the world wouldn't have kept them apart.

He just couldn't help being upset about the lost years.

He wanted to make up for them.

Wanted to learn about her, talk to her, work with her, and build a life with her.

Which was crazy, since they just started talking to each other earlier that day.

He told himself to put the brakes on those thoughts and let things play out the way they needed to. A foundation that was hastily constructed wasn't usually the kind of foundation that lasted through a lot of storms and years.

And that's the kind of foundation he wanted with Brooklyn. One that was going to last forever. So he pulled his thoughts away from Brooklyn and the relationship he wanted to have with her and tried to focus on the reason that they had reconciled to begin with. Quinn.

"What about Quinn—"

"We should talk about Quinn—"

They looked over at each other and laughed at both of them talking at the same time.

The line about great minds thinking alike drifted through his head, but he didn't say that. He didn't necessarily think he had a great mind, but maybe minds that were meant to be together, or minds that were compatible, minds that were made to spend a lifetime together, thought alike.

There he was, thinking about forever again, and romance, wanting all the things, when he barely had two pennies to rub together and he needed to tell Brooklyn about that.

Quinn first.

"Go ahead. You start," Brooklyn nudged when he didn't say anything.

"I think we're gonna start the same conversation. What are we going to do with Quinn. What are we going to do with ourselves when we go to meet Quinn?"

"You're saying are we going to be married tomorrow?"

She didn't sound like the idea was repulsive to her. In fact, she almost sounded like she was laughing. Like the idea of them deciding to get married the next day was slightly funny.

He had to agree. He certainly would never have seen himself getting married so quickly to anyone. Let alone to Brooklyn.

"Yeah. I guess I'm asking. I... I can see the benefits both ways."

"Me too. I suppose being married when we get her will allow us to be in the same house together, acting as mom and dad—"

"*Being* mom and dad," he corrected gently. They weren't going to *act* like anything. They were going to be parents. It was a small distinction but one he wanted to make. This wasn't something that he was pretending. This was real life.

She nodded, almost as though she understood exactly what he was saying and the distinction he was trying to make.

Minds that were meant to be together thought the same. That wasn't the way the saying went, but he felt like he needed to rewrite that one.

"Yes. So, we would be her parents from the very start. There wouldn't be any more adjusting for her. It would give her the most solid, structured foundation we possibly can. Of course, there would be you and me kind of adjusting to our relationship, and that might affect her."

"Maybe we could do that behind closed doors. After all, I feel like we've been pretty mature lately." He grinned about that because he was complimenting them both. But he did. He felt like they had handled this the best way a person possibly could. Maybe that was arrogant, and he didn't want to be prideful, but he felt like they could have been more concerned about themselves and how this was going to affect their lives, but he felt like both of them had put Quinn first. Which was the way it should be.

"If we can put Quinn first when we're shocked and taken aback, put her welfare above our own, I'm pretty sure it's not going to be that hard to do the same thing when we're at home, adjusting."

"I think you might be right. I hope you are. And she'll be at school for a few weeks, anyway, and both you and I work from home, so we'll have plenty of time to talk when she's not there if we need to."

Brooklyn didn't seem like the kind of person who got angry and spouted off without thinking about it.

She'd been angry with him for a long time, and she'd never erupted in a tantrum.

And now that they'd figured out that they could talk to each other and work out a lot of things that they might not understand otherwise, maybe they'd get along even better than they might have without knowing.

"So, I was wondering why we had to dislike each other for so long. Why we couldn't have figured this out and fixed it years ago? Back in high school. Right away. If I would have realized what was going on. If I had paid better attention, instead of being so wrapped up in myself. We could have talked it out. And not wasted all these years."

"Yeah. That's a good point."

"But then, the thought came to me that maybe we needed to have those years. That time that was wasted because neither one of us was willing to go to the other and discuss what happened. There was no communication. And no relationship. Maybe that was a lesson, as hard as it was, and as long as it took, that we needed to learn before we got Quinn."

"That's interesting. I thought about the wasted years too. But I thought about my stupidity in not...confronting you. Although I don't think I was brave enough to do that. I thought you hated me. I thought all those things I heard were things that you said. So, you're right. I can definitely learn from that. If I had confronted you about them, and you had been rude to me, that would have been better than believing a lie for fifteen years."

He waited for another car to pass, putting the high beams back on before he said, "I guess we should just make sure we're on the same page. I assume Quinn is going to need counseling or something. Especially if the grandmother can't stay."

"It would be nice if we could find a counselor close so we don't have to go to the Cities... Once a week?"

"Probably. I would think it would be at least that much, but I agree. That might be one change that would be a good idea to make. Not only will it disrupt our schedules, but I don't think I've ever met a little kid who enjoys a long car ride, especially on a weekly basis."

Brooklyn laughed a little, and he figured she agreed with him. As a kid, he'd hated any time he had to get in the car and drive more than about five minutes.

"I agree with that. Maybe they'll have something set up already, but if they don't, I think that would be our first order of business. And if they don't have a counselor?"

"Maybe we'll see how she is. See how she seems to be doing. I think... I just think that being in a stable environment, having whatever fear she has, if any, addressed, and giving her a firm foundation in the Bible, where she knows that God loves her and will never leave her. That might be the very best thing we can do for her, even above and beyond counseling."

"I agree," she said, and she sounded a little surprised.

Her words, said low, but with feeling, made him feel like maybe they really did have the same values after all. It would be kind of hard to raise children if he was trying to teach them that God loved them, and she was trying to take them to a secular counselor to tell them they could find the power within themselves and be steeped in humanism.

"I... I need to tell you something," she said, and he got the feeling that she was changing the subject.

"Okay." It also reminded him that he needed to talk to her about the finances of his ranch. He didn't want her to think that she was marrying a prosperous rancher, when he was one that was barely holding on by his fingernails.

"I keep the books for my sisters and me on the ranch. You know it's been a hard couple of years, with the blight we had on the wheat and then a drought last summer. We got plenty of rain and snow over the winter to make up for it, but that didn't change the fact that there was not enough to feed all of our stock, and we had to sell some."

"You and me both."

Her head jerked over, surprise in her eyes, then a bit of an understanding darkened them, and he figured that his news wasn't going to be quite as surprising to her as what he thought it might be. And in fact, he was getting the feeling that she had the exact same news of her own.

"Our baking business has been growing slowly, and we have the potential to have several new clients, including this one that we're going to tonight. But...if things don't change, and in a rather big way, we could end up losing the ranch." She took a breath before she hurried on. "My sisters don't know. Not how bad it is. They know that things are tight, and we're saving every penny, not spending anything that we don't have to, but they don't know that we're not actually making our payments and we're getting more and more behind."

"Wow. And you're carrying this alone?"

"I can't burden them with it. I just...can't."

"Maybe you should." He squeezed her hand, where his still sat on it on her leg. And this time, she turned her hand around, and their fingers twined together, a feeling that he loved and that made him feel...less alone somehow.

"I suppose I should. If it were me, and I've thought about this an awful lot, I would want to know. I would be upset if the ranch was in such a state and whoever was taking care of the bills didn't tell me. But at the same time, with all the stress we already have, I know that that stress on top of that isn't good for them. It will possibly contribute to health problems and other issues, and I didn't want to make life any harder on my sisters than what I have to. So, while I usually try to do unto others as I would have them do unto me, in this case, I felt like I was protecting their health by not saying anything... Is that terrible?"

He had to shake his head. He understood. "I see what you're doing. I...admire that. You care about them, and your concern is for their health and for their general welfare. And not knowing isn't going to hurt anything. It's not like they can do anything more than what they're already doing."

"Exactly. If telling them would help in some other way, I would gladly do it, but it won't. So, I'm not going to."

"You have to eventually. How long do you have?"

"Without a major drastic change, by fall."

That was just a few months. That wasn't much time.

"It's tempting to me to hold back on the information I need to tell you, for the same reasons, but since we're not married, I feel like you need to know before you make the decision to go through with the marriage. That might be better for you."

"Well, I guess I've already said it, but I'll repeat it. I would rather know than not." She shrugged. "As a wife too. After all, if I keep the books for the farm, you don't want me keeping that information from you, do you?"

"No. I... I'll have to fight myself on that one. Maybe it won't be an issue. But right now, it is. I went through the same drought you guys did. I had the same blight on my wheat. I'm struggling as well. I hired the flyboys over on Sweet Briar Ranch to do my crop dusting, in hopes that spending that money will be worth it, since I won't have the blight to deal with. Leafhoppers took a lot of my alfalfa, and that's the main thing I'm having them dust for. Anyway, I hope the investment is worth it. Beyond that, things have been really tight in my area too. I didn't want you to think you're marrying a prosperous rancher."

"I guess I don't care about money, but we do need to have enough to pay our bills. Maybe two people with money problems shouldn't be thinking about joining forces?" She didn't sound like she was saying she didn't believe they should, she was asking, and he shook his head immediately.

"No. If we were both incapable of handling money, I would say that might be a good idea. But neither one of us could control the blight or the drought or the leafhoppers. So, my opinion is that's not an issue."

He wanted her to agree with him. He didn't want her to say that she was changing her mind and thought they ought not to go ahead with what they were going to do.

He couldn't believe how strongly he felt about it. But it was true. He didn't want her to change her mind and decide they shouldn't get married after all.

"I agree. That makes sense, and it wouldn't matter if both of us were incapable of handling money. If even one of us has to buy everything we see, the other one shouldn't be considering marrying them."

He nodded. He knew people like that. People who were incapable of telling themselves no or making themselves wait. He hadn't thought that Brooklyn was that kind of person, but he agreed with her that being married to a person like that would be a constant struggle and probably constant arguing as well.

"I guess you figured out that your financial situation doesn't make a difference to me."

She hadn't said anything, and so he felt like he needed to announce that and hope that she felt the same.

"The only thing I'm concerned about is Quinn's stability. I don't want to lose the ranch and have her home yanked out from underneath her again."

"We should emphasize the importance of God. That God allows us to go through trials. That He gives us hardships to endure to make us stronger. That sometimes He takes something away from us, because He wants us to turn our attention to something else. Or in my case, anyway, He gives me something, like to have custody of a little girl, so that I can finally see the woman I was meant to be looking at."

She didn't say anything for a moment, but her breath seemed to catch in her throat while her hand tightened on his.

He hoped he hadn't been pushing her too hard. He was saying the truth. Even if he hadn't even articulated that thought in his head before the words came out of his mouth.

But really, God had given him Quinn, and he believed that part of the reason was not just to provide a home for Quinn but to draw him to Brooklyn. After all, he liked her a long time ago, but he'd allowed that feeling to stagnate, doing nothing about it because of the rift between them. The arrival of Quinn had made him face everything they hadn't been willing to face before.

"Now that you've mentioned it, I suppose that's true for me as well. I hadn't considered that, but God does have a way of arranging our lives. Although I certainly would never tell Quinn that God had arranged her life in such a way so that she could meet us. Because I'm not sure that we can explain the death of her parents quite that lightly."

"For sure. I'm not sure how to explain that, other than we just have to trust God and know that His ways are best. Even though we live in a fallen world, with sin rampant around us, and death because of the sin of man, God will give us victory if we trust in Him."

"Yeah. I agree. And I agree that those are the things that we need to be teaching Quinn, not to base her life on a ranch, or her security on where we live, or even who lives with her, although I hope she can have security in our relationship and not be worried that it's not strong or won't last."

"That's going to be my priority too. A relationship with you, and teaching Quinn to have a relationship with God. I think that's the best thing we can do for her."

"I agree."

"So...does that mean we should get married in the morning?" He hesitated to ask, because he didn't want to push, but that was the direction his thoughts had gone. He felt like whatever they did, Brooklyn and he were mature enough to handle it. Maybe they would never fall in love, maybe they would never have a passionate relationship, but they would have a strong one. Built on a godly and biblical foundation.

"I always read the story of Rebecca and Isaac in the Bible, and I wondered how Rebecca could leave her home and travel so far away, knowing she might never see her family again, and then meet Isaac, and be married to him...maybe right away?" She shook her head. "And yet here I am."

"You've known me for a lot longer than Rebecca knew Isaac," he teased her a little, squeezing her hand, and she grinned up at him, but there was still some uncertainty and fear in her eyes. "The thing that always struck me about that story was they went through a lot of pains to find a woman who believed the same way they did. I felt like that was always God saying that it was more important to find someone who believed in God, who was a committed Christian, who wasn't like the world around you, than it was for you to be 'in love.'" He used his fingers to put air quotes around the words "in love."

"That's a good point. I guess I hadn't really considered that. I'd always read that story from the perspective of Rebecca and just wondering if I could ever have that kind of faith. I feel like I couldn't. I mean, she didn't know what kind of man Isaac was. He could have been anyone."

"Isaac could have been getting someone that he didn't care for either," he reminded her.

"Sure, but he at least knew the servant who was picking her out. He might have given the servant a few last-minute instructions. You know, please make sure she's pretty. Please don't pick out one that doesn't get up until dinnertime and gossips all day."

"Do you really think those are the things that Isaac was concerned about?" he asked, humor in his tone.

"I hope so," she said, but her eyes were glinting back at him, and they shared a little humor without saying anything else at all.

Five minutes later, they hadn't said anything more, and Brooklyn directed him to take the exit off the highway. He couldn't believe how fast the time had flown by with them talking together. He wondered if they would always have that kind of communication. The kind where he felt like he could talk to her forever and time flew by without him even realizing it.

Content to sit with his hand in hers, with the night flying by around them, with nothing but the headlights ahead. He realized he hadn't been that content in a very long time.

All the things that he had said to her, the things about God working things out so that he would know that communication was important, about both of them having financial issues on their farms and in their personal lives, and then acknowledging that they would want to talk about those things after they were married, that neither one of them would want to have those things kept from them. All the hardship seemed to make sense. Not that it made it easier, but he could see God's hand working, bringing things together.

He wasn't quite sure how Quinn fit into everything, but he hadn't even met her, and he loved her like a daughter. Wanting the very best for her, without even knowing her.

Brooklyn spent the rest of the trip giving him instructions on which turns to take, and they made it to the grocery store without incident. Brooklyn had texted the owner to let him know what time they were getting there, and he met them at the side door. They helped unload the car, and the owner told Brooklyn he'd pay the invoice when she sent it. She thanked him for coming, and they got back in the car to drive home.

Cormac hated to push, but he knew he needed to talk to her and at least get something set up for their marriage.

But she spoke before he could.

"Can we meet at the courthouse at nine o'clock? I don't think there's a waiting period of any kind. All we have to do is find someone who's willing to marry us once we have a license."

"I know the pastor would do it. He knows us both, and he married Smith and Abrielle, and they were doing basically the same thing we were, only we're doing it for a child."

"I'd be lying, at this point, if I said that the only reason I am reminding you of this is because of Quinn. Of course, I wouldn't want to rush into anything, but...you definitely are someone I would be interested in without a child between us."

His heart stuttered at her words. His mind raced, even as his lips smiled. He wanted to hear that. Wanted that to be true. And appreciated the fact that she said it without him having to prompt her in any way.

"I guess I don't know exactly where we are in our relationship, and maybe it doesn't matter right now. But I agree with you. I told you I regretted the years that we wasted, and that was mostly because I feel like you're perfect for me. I feel like you were perfect for me fifteen years ago, and I wasn't very smart."

"But you said God has a plan, and I agree. He definitely worked things out, and while we might see those years as wasted, I think they're more like learning opportunities, opportunities for us to grow, opportunities for us to appreciate each other more than we would have if we had been together when we were so young."

"I agree. And the time sounds good. Nine o'clock at the courthouse." He reached in the cupholder where he put his phone and handed it to Brooklyn. He gave her his password. "Do you mind getting the pastor's number for me? Please? It might be a little late, but if he doesn't answer tonight, I'll call him in the morning. I believe the letter said Quinn was coming at ten, so we don't have much time." He looked down, his hands tightening on the wheel. He hadn't put his hand back on her lap, and she cradled his phone in hers. "I kind of hate that. I haven't really experienced it, but I understand that women seem to like to make a big deal about their wedding. And that's not something you're going to be able to do, considering that in twelve hours from now, we're planning on being married."

"Wow." She stopped, dropping her hand into her lap with his phone clenched in her fingers. "That really makes it real." She sounded a little breathless.

"It's not too late to change your mind. We don't have to do this. I don't want you to feel like you don't have a choice or that I'm pushing you into something you don't want."

"You don't have to say that again. You aren't pushing me into anything. In fact, if I recall correctly, I'm the one who brought it up just now. I'm fine without a big, fancy wedding. I've never needed fancy to be happy. But it's a huge commitment. I feel a little breathless just thinking about it. Not breathless that I'm terrified and don't want to do it, just breathless in this is a huge step, and I recognize the enormity of it."

"Yeah. My stomach feels a little empty, just like it doesn't have any gravity. It's floating. And I think that's kind of the same thing." He nodded at the phone. "Still, if we're going to get the preacher, we need to do it."

She pressed the buttons and got the call set up on hands-free. It seemed a little anticlimactic when the pastor answered and agreed immediately to preside over the wedding. At first expressing a bit of surprise, then chuckling and saying that he had been shocked by Smith and Abrielle, but maybe it was some kind of disease that was floating around Sweet Water. He asked them to come a little early so that he could go through some counseling with them, and Cormac agreed to be there as soon as they could after they got their license, with the pastor understanding that they needed to be at his ranch by ten.

"If we can't do marriage counseling tomorrow, we'll do it sometime. I think it's important."

They nodded and agreed, and just like that, they planned to get married in the morning.

Cormac knew they were making the right decision, but he just hoped that he was able to be the husband that she deserved. And the father that Quinn needed.

Chapter 15

"You look beautiful," Teagan said as she held Brooklyn's hands out in front of her in her own, looking at her with such love in her eyes that Brooklyn felt tears prick hers.

She hadn't even told her parents that she was getting married. She would eventually announce that she'd tied the knot, but neither one of them were going to come from where they were on such short notice. She probably would take some flack from her mom, because although they weren't close, her mom still got offended if she wasn't one of the first people to know the things that were going on in their lives.

Over the years, she and her sisters had argued over who had to call and tell their mom different things that had gone on, and they tried to make a weekly call to both even when there wasn't much of anything happening.

She didn't want the added stress of a phone call that probably wasn't going to be super pleasant, so she hadn't talked to her mother. So Teagan's words and her look of absolute love were like rain on parched ground in her heart.

Zaylee and Ainsley both stood on either side of her as well, telling her that Cormac was a lucky man, and she was beautiful, and of course that they would miss her.

She would be moving into Cormac's house, they figured that much out, because of Quinn, but when she would be coming to get the rest of her stuff, or how she would still be working with her sisters, was yet to be determined.

She just knew that she was close enough to make the drive every day and expected to, although she wouldn't be able to start until after Quinn had been safely deposited on the school bus.

She had chosen to wear a flowing light green blouse with ties up the front and a bit of a ruffle around the sleeves. It fit around her waist and dressed up the jeans and cowgirl boots she wore.

She wasn't going to have time to change, and they were going to have Quinn, so she figured a fancy dress was out of the question. Not that she had very many fancy dresses to choose from. She had a couple of dresses left from high school and one or two that she had worn as a bridesmaid in different weddings and just hadn't gotten taken to the thrift store to be dropped off yet.

Plus, this outfit probably was a lot more practical, and at heart, while she loved the idea of being a princess, she was a practical girl.

"Are you sure we can't come?" Ainsley asked for what felt like the millionth time.

"No. You're already going to be late for the farmers market, and we're just going to the pastor's to get marriage counseling and to have a quick exchange of vows. There isn't going to be anything fancy about it, and then we're going to have to hurry to the ranch and get Quinn."

"I just hate seeing you do it all by yourself." Zaylee put her arm around her.

"I don't mind. And plus, I'm hardly going to be getting married by myself. The pastor and Cormac will be there."

"You know what I meant," Zaylee said, and while she returned Brooklyn's smile, there was still sadness in her eyes.

Brooklyn hadn't meant to spring everything on them quite as quickly as she had; it had been sprung on her just as fast. She understood that it took a little time to adjust.

"Change is never easy," she said. "But you guys know that I think this is exactly what God wants me to do. And to not do it would be worse than the discomfort that we're feeling now as things shift around us."

They nodded in agreement, and she hugged each one of them before she grabbed the bag she packed, with a few extra outfits and all the toiletries she would need to get her through a week, although she expected to be back far before that, and headed out to her car.

The last time she walked out of the house as a single woman.

She couldn't let her mind dwell on those thoughts though, or she'd be crying before she made it to the ceremony.

Cormac would think she didn't want to marry him. And although that was not true, he would be right to be concerned, because she wanted there to be more than friendship between them. She was hoping the relationship would grow into more. And while she hadn't said that last night, she felt that maybe she should have. They should have talked about where they expected their relationship to go and not just what they expected to happen with Quinn.

But Cormac had proven to be an easy person to talk to, and she felt like they would have time to discuss that at some point.

The drive into town seemed to take no time at all, and before she knew it, she was pulling up to the courthouse in Rockerton, seeing Cormac already standing at the steps waiting on her.

She got out of her car and walked over to him as he walked to her, his arms out.

He was going to hug her.

She realized that with a few seconds to spare, to prepare herself.

It would take more than a few seconds to prepare herself for Cormac's hug. He had talked about how she had smelled nice; she could say the exact same thing back to him. It was a scent that she wasn't used to, but she didn't know a lot about men's cologne. Maybe that was it. He did look freshly shaved.

But the feel of his arms around her, being pressed up against a solid warmth, gave her strength and fortitude that she didn't know she was lacking or needed.

"I hadn't realized how nervous I was until you put your arms around me and made my anxiety go away."

"We'd look kind of funny walking into the courthouse like this, but we can if it'll make you feel better."

She laughed. Loved that even on a day like today where she was taking one of the biggest steps of her life and doing it with less than twenty-four hours of thought, he could make her laugh and feel almost...carefree.

She supposed, since she had found a man who could make her laugh in such circumstances, she was wise to be marrying him. A man like that was certainly one worth keeping. Especially when he was a hard worker and had character and integrity as well.

She was getting a man who was worth taking risks for.

It didn't take much time at all to get the license. The clerk at the courthouse didn't know them and didn't act surprised to see two people who had been enemies all their lives holding hands and signing their names, announcing their intent to be married.

Surprised to see it was already 9:25 when they stepped out of the courthouse, she looked up at Cormac. "Are we going to be able to make it out to the ranch in time?"

"Yeah. I just texted the pastor, and he's waiting for us. I'm sure he's not going to forget about the marriage counseling he wants us to do, but we'll stop in quick and get married fast." He side-eyed her. "I'm sorry about that."

She shook her head. "It's necessary. And I'm totally with you. After all, you're getting cheated too."

"I didn't grow up dreaming about my wedding. I did grow up dreaming about my wife..." He let that sentence trail off, and she had a feeling that he might have said more. That he wasn't just dreaming about his wife but about being married. "Anyway, we'll have some time to spare. A few minutes if everything goes well. We might be slightly late if we get behind a tractor or have to wait for a moose to cross the road."

She laughed. That had happened. The moose, although the tractor was more likely, but sometimes in North Dakota, odd things happened.

He was right about the time to spare. It was five 'til ten when they pulled into his ranch.

"Is it terrible that I don't feel married?" she asked, looking ahead out the windshield as he pulled into the parking area and stopped.

They had decided to take one vehicle, since it would be faster instead of trying to maneuver around with two.

That just meant they needed to take another trip to Rockerton and pick her car up at some point. Although she had thrown her things in the back of his, so it wasn't something that had to happen that day.

"Everything happened so quickly," he murmured. "I don't blame you. I don't really feel married either. And we should have stopped and gotten rings. But I didn't think about that either. I wish we had some way of contacting these people and letting them know that we needed a few more hours."

She laughed. But she had to agree. Just a few more hours would have given them enough time to be able to take two vehicles and to stop and get rings and to engage in the marriage counseling the pastor wanted them to.

"I suppose this is just a test of our ability to roll with things," she said. "But a ring would definitely help me feel like this is real."

"When we go to pick up your car, we'll make sure we get one." He hesitated and then said quickly, "Two. Or three. An engagement ring and wedding ring for you. And a wedding band for me as well."

It made her feel good that he wanted to wear a ring. Some men didn't. But she supposed she wanted people to know that he was married just as much as she was.

Chapter 16

Cormac worked to keep his hands from trembling as he put them behind Brooklyn's back to guide her into his house.

He'd spent a couple of hours that morning tidying things up, sweeping and scrubbing and dusting. Moving his things around so they looked less cluttered and more like a home that there was room for a woman in.

He wasn't deluding himself that she might feel comfortable here. There weren't any of the knickknacks that he figured women liked. The walls were plain, with just a calendar in the kitchen and nothing else. But the countertops were cleaned off, the dishes were done and put away, and the floor was clean.

She looked around as she walked in, and he wished he could see it from her eyes. For him, it was cleaner than it had been for months, but even as he thought that, his eyes caught on a cobweb in the corner, and he figured that it probably wasn't even close to meeting her cleanliness standards.

"I tried to clean up. I can see that I didn't do a very good job. There's a cobweb in the corner. I wish it were better for you."

She turned, looking him in the eye, with her brows drawn. "There's nothing wrong. If you would have had to move your previous girlfriend out before I could move in, that would be a problem. A few cobwebs and bare walls don't bother me at all."

He snorted at her reasoning, but it made him smile. He had made a pretty big gamble on this woman, and he felt like everything she did justified the risk he had taken. After all, she had just stood there in front of him and told him the things that were important and the things that were not.

He couldn't argue or fault her, and he appreciated that her heart was set on God's things, not the world's.

"Let me show you around upstairs, I...had a few extra bedsheets and I got two rooms ready. We should talk about how we were going to handle bedrooms between you and me, but I assumed that you want your own, at least for a bit."

She didn't say anything, and he wished he wouldn't have made her a bedroom of her own. He got the feeling that she would have been willing to share his.

He made it halfway up the stairs before he decided that he was going to say something. Once Quinn came, it wasn't going to be something he was going to be comfortable talking about unless Quinn wasn't around.

"Would you rather share my room?" he asked, slowing but not stopping as he led her up the stairs.

"That might be best. That would avoid the awkwardness of having to move at some point. I don't know how long—"

"Not long."

"Oh."

He'd shocked her. He hadn't meant to.

"I wasn't sure exactly where our relationship was, and I guess with all the other things we talked about, it wasn't something I thought to ask until last night as I lay in bed. Wondering what was going to happen."

"I don't want to rush into anything. But I do intend to have a real marriage. With all the things that that entails." His brows drew down a little. He hadn't even considered anything else. Maybe she had?

"Okay. I just wasn't sure how you felt about me exactly."

"And you about me. It's not just my feelings."

"No. But I know my feelings. I didn't know yours."

"And yours are?" He got to the top of the stairs and wanted to wait for her to answer, but he knew they didn't have much time.

So, when she didn't answer right away, he walked to the first bedroom on the right.

"This is Quinn's bedroom." He opened the door so she could look in. There was a bed, which he had made with clean sheets. And there was a dresser with a mirror over top of it. Not much else.

He wasn't sure exactly what a seven-year-old needed, but he figured a place to stay and sleep and a place to keep her clothes was probably a good start.

"This looks perfect." That was all Brooklyn said.

He pointed to the left as they stepped out. "There are two spare bedrooms right there. One on the left, one on the right, and the bathroom's at the end of the hall. I was going to give you the bedroom on the left, the one right beside Quinn. And if the grandmother stays, she'd get the room across the hall."

He moved to his right and walked down a few paces. "This is my room. And if you think it's a good idea for us to start out together here, I agree. It's the only bedroom that has a master bath, although there's no tub, just a shower."

"Anything that will get me clean will work." She worried her bottom lip with her teeth. "Are you sure you're okay with that?"

"It would be my preference. I didn't want to push you."

"Then let's do it that way. I'm not sure how I feel about the sleeping arrangements, but we can talk about that later. I think I hear a vehicle."

He tilted his head, surprised that she had heard it before him.

"I'd say that's them," he said after checking his watch.

"All right. Let me throw these in here, and then I guess it's show-time." Her lips pulled back, but her smile didn't look humorous, more nervous than anything.

"It's okay. We're going to make it through this, doing it together. I know we'll laugh at this someday." He hoped that was true.

She stepped inside the door he pushed open and set her bags down, then stood, and she was smiling. "I believe you're right. I think this is going to be quite funny at some point. And our kids are going to laugh at us."

Kids. More than Quinn. There would be other kids.

Of course he'd thought about that. But...to hear her say it, to talk about them like they were here. It made his stomach do some kind of odd tumble where it seemed to bump up against his heart and lungs and liver until his insides felt all jumbled up.

They walked down the stairs together, her in front, and maybe it was his imagination, but he thought her feet dragged as she walked to the door.

She opened it before anyone knocked, and he followed her out, standing on the porch as the occupants of the car that had just parked beside his truck got out.

An older gentleman, dressed in a suit, got out of the driver's side. He looked sufficiently boring for Cormac to decide he was the lawyer.

An elderly woman, surely the grandmother, sat in the passenger side and got out slowly, leaning heavily on her walker.

She looked like a typical grandma. All she needed was an apron and some flour on her cheek for him to think that she would be just like the grandmas of his imagination.

But his attention did not stay long on the two adults in front but was diverted, as though pulled by an invisible string, toward the little girl getting out of the back.

She didn't seem unnecessarily sad, although she did move slower than he would have thought a child would move.

Of course, he was used to boys. As a child, he never walked if he could run. And he never ran if he could go faster.

Girls were slightly different, and he supposed he was going to have to get used to that. Figure it out. The idea gave him some fear before he remembered that he had Brooklyn beside him, and she had been a little girl once. Surely figuring out little girls would be easier for someone who used to be one.

Quinn was cute, with light brown hair that fell down her back in straight lines. Her eyes were serious, looking around her, taking everything in, before they fell on him.

He felt when she was looking at him that she was trying to figure him out too.

Then her eyes went to Brooklyn, and for the first time, the little lips turned up.

Cormac found that he wasn't the slightest bit jealous; the only feeling in his chest was happiness. If Quinn developed a tight and beautiful bond with Brooklyn, he would be their biggest cheerleader. He wanted to see them get along and have a great relationship.

He wouldn't begrudge it at all; it could only be the very best thing that could happen to Quinn and probably one of the best things that could happen to Brooklyn too.

Hopefully, having a relationship with her husband would be the best thing that could happen to Brooklyn, but he would be working on that.

"You must be Mr. Henderson," the man said, holding his hand out, his stride surprisingly spry for a man of his age.

"I am." Cormac walked down the stairs, his own hand clasping the lawyer's and shaking it.

"I'm Colby Jones of Jones and Jones law offices, and I see you got my letter. At least you're standing on your porch like you're expecting us."

"I did, *we* did, and we are."

"I take it that's Brooklyn Lepley?" the lawyer said, nodding at Brooklyn.

Brooklyn had taken the steps more slowly than he had, but she reached his side just at that moment and held her hand out. "Yes. I'm Brooklyn. Pleased to meet you."

The man grabbed her hand, introducing himself again, and then he nodded at the older lady who was slowly making her way around the car.

“This is Karen. She’s Quinn’s maternal grandmother. She’s been taking care of her, but as you can see, she’s not getting around well enough to be chasing after a seven-year-old. She was hoping that you would be able to let her stay here for a few weeks until Quinn is settled in.”

“We were hoping she would stay. We’re fine if she stays permanently. We’ve already talked about it, and our home is open if she would like to make herself a place here.”

“Well, why, my goodness,” the old lady said. “I was not expecting that. I thought I would have to beg to stay for a bit.” She put her hand on her heart.

“I hope not. If Quinn loves you, then we love you too. And you’re welcome here for as long as you want.” He glanced at Brooklyn, who was nodding, smiling at Miss Karen.

She moved forward, her hand out. “I’m so happy to meet you. I’m Brooklyn.”

Karen stood still, taking her hand off her walker and holding it out for Brooklyn to shake. “I wondered what you would look like. Kendra talked highly of you, and I guess I shouldn’t be surprised at the hospitality that you guys are showing a complete stranger. So old-fashioned, and I appreciate it.”

“It’s Biblical. And I hope we would extend it to anyone,” Brooklyn said, and Cormac couldn’t be more proud of her. That’s exactly what he would have said if he had been thinking. But she spoke for him, and her words were exactly what he would have wanted her to say.

But as much as he was happy to meet the lawyer and Miss Karen, Quinn was the one he most wanted to be introduced to. His eyes were drawn to her as she came around and stood solemnly between the lawyer and her grandmother.

Without thinking about it, he went down on one knee. "You must be Quinn."

She nodded. "And you must be Mr. Cormac. I don't have to call you dad. Grandma said so."

"No. You most certainly do not. I do however hope that you'll be okay to tell me if you need anything or if there's anything I can do for you."

"Everyone's been really nice to me since my parents died. I'm not a baby. I can do things on my own."

Cormac nodded, his brows going up. Maybe she was tired of people pandering to her and wanted to push back, showing that she could be autonomous.

Or maybe she was afraid to get attached to anyone.

Brooklyn hunkered down beside him, and without thinking about it, he put an arm around her to steady her.

"I'm Brooklyn. I was a friend of your mom's."

"Mom talked about you before she died. She told me that you might be my mom someday, but Dad got sick before he could ask you to marry him."

That was news to Brooklyn apparently. He could feel the shiver that went through her. One of surprise, he assumed, but maybe repulsion. It seemed like she had lots of offers of marriage, but none because a man had fallen in love with her. Just because he wanted her as a mother to this child.

Cormac tucked that away to examine a little closer later. He didn't want her thinking that that was all she was worth. Just someone to be a mother. He... He might not have been jolted out of his complacency without Quinn, but he didn't need Quinn in order to see what an amazing woman Brooklyn was. He didn't know much about people, women in particular, but he knew he didn't want to be wanted just for his ranch or just for something else that he had. He wanted his wife to look at him and admire him as a man. For himself.

He wanted to do the same thing for Brooklyn.

"It looks like God worked it out that I could be your mom anyway," Brooklyn said softly.

Cormac noted that Quinn seemed to be okay with Brooklyn being her mom but had specifically told him that he was not going to be her dad.

He didn't take offense at that. Her dad was the one who had just passed away. Maybe she had healed from her mother's death, enough to want a new mother anyway, and maybe her dad's death was too fresh.

Whatever it was, he wasn't going to let a seven-year-old offend him. He was going to love her no matter what she said.

It would be nice if it were easy, since this was a big change for them all, but if she proved to be difficult, he could not fault her, considering what she'd been through.

"Would you like us to take you inside and show you around the house?" Brooklyn asked, holding out her hand.

Quinn's brows raised a little, almost as though she wasn't sure she could trust Brooklyn.

"It's okay, sweetie. Remember, we said that these two people are going to be taking care of you. Now, they said that Grandma could stay, and I will if they really mean it. And we have to learn to love them," Miss Karen counseled Quinn, and to Cormac's relief, she seemed to be encouraging the little girl to trust Brooklyn and him. He couldn't know exactly how the lady felt, but she seemed to want the best for the little girl as well. That could only make everything easier all the way around.

"How about you show Quinn around, and then we'll all sit down at the kitchen table. I have some papers we need to go over and sign, and I have some other instructions that Quinn's parents wanted me to read. I see there aren't any neighbors and no other children around?" He left that as a question and raised his brows at Cormac.

"No. We're pretty isolated out here. Closest house is a mile away."

He hoped that didn't have any bearing on whether or not they would be able to keep Quinn.

"All right. I was hoping she might be able to play with some new friends, but we'll have to distract her somehow, because I'm sure that she's not going to want to sit and listen to the adults talk about the boring things that lawyers have to talk about on a daily basis."

The man smiled as he spoke and looked down affectionately at Quinn. Cormac got the impression that maybe he had met her a few times, and while the man didn't exactly seem like he was great with children, he seemed like he truly had a deep affection for Quinn.

It wasn't hard to see why as Quinn grabbed Brooklyn's hand, and they walked up the steps together. Cormac offered his arm to Miss Karen and carried her walker in one hand as they went more slowly up the stairs.

"She's been through a lot, as I'm sure you know," Karen started speaking as they walked up the steps. "I'm sure it's not going to surprise you that she might be a little bit frosty to begin with, but she's been such a happy and sweet child. Even with losing her mom, even with her dad being sick. I hate to see her going through so much, and I'm not sure how much of a mark it's going to leave on her."

"It's sure to mark her somehow," Cormac said.

"I know. Sad but true. So, I'm going to do my best to try to ease the transition as much as I can. I talked really well about both of you, tried to get her excited about meeting you. Tried to make sure that she knew that you were doing this for her good and wanted only the best for her. I hoped I was right." The woman paused as Cormac opened the door and set her walker in front of her. "I feel like I was."

The woman walked in, and Cormac continued to hold the door as the lawyer made his way in as well. He didn't say anything, just nodded his head. It stood to reason that he wouldn't know the family very well, despite the fact that he seemed to have somewhat of a relationship with Quinn.

Glad that he'd already had a chance to show Brooklyn around the house, he stood in the kitchen with Miss Karen and the lawyer as Brooklyn and Quinn stomped around upstairs. He could hear Brooklyn's voice occasionally as she showed Quinn the bathroom and the bedrooms, and heard the door shut as they must have exited, then the footsteps on the stairs as they came back down.

"I don't watch much TV, but we could probably turn on her favorite show if you know what it is?" Cormac said to Miss Karen.

"I don't need to sit in here and listen, either. If you show me your TV and teach me how to work your remote, I'm sure we can find something that will keep us occupied until the adults are done talking."

Cormac nodded at the lawyer to let him know that he'd be right back, and then he led Miss Karen into the living room where his small TV was located.

As he was explaining how to use the remote to Miss Karen, his eyes caught on Brooklyn as she walked in behind Quinn.

Her eyes weren't exactly glowing, but there was a small smile on her face, and Quinn's hand was still safely entrusted to hers.

That eased Cormac's mind more than he could believe it would, and he thought that maybe they were going to be able to do this thing after all.

Chapter 17

The porch swing creaked as Brooklyn sat beside Cormac, their clasped hands sitting on the swing between them.

She wasn't sure when holding hands with Cormac had become something that felt natural, but it had.

Quinn sat on the other side of Brooklyn, her head leaning against her side, with Brooklyn's arm around her.

Her soft, even breathing indicated that she had fallen asleep.

"It was a big day for her," Brooklyn said softly.

"And for you."

"And you," Brooklyn said, humor in her tone as they tossed the verbal ball back and forth.

"And for Miss Karen, but apparently she couldn't take it, since she went to bed an hour and a half ago."

"We'll see how early you go to bed when you're her age," Brooklyn said in Miss Karen's defense.

Miss Karen had been amazing. She hadn't seemed to be jealous or possessive of Quinn and did not seem to resent Brooklyn taking what used to be her daughter's place in Quinn's life. She just seemed to want whatever was best for Quinn. Brooklyn figured that if there were more people like Miss Karen in the world, life would be better for everyone.

Regardless, she loved the old lady and was glad that she was going to try to make arrangements to stay there permanently. She had a house to sell and some other things to take care of back in the Cities, but with Cormac and Brooklyn helping her, she had said that she didn't think it would be hard to do.

She had offered to pay rent, which Cormac had declined immediately. But the lady had been insistent and had written a check out.

It was not a huge amount, but Brooklyn figured it would probably ease a little bit of the financial strain that they were under.

Miss Karen had said that she was paying to stay at her house, and she needed to do something with her moldy money.

That had made both Brooklyn and Cormac smile, because they both figured that she didn't have a problem finding places to spend her money.

But they didn't argue.

That really wasn't the big financial news of the day, though.

Nelson arrives tomorrow.

"Can you believe they get so much money for stud fees from a horse?" Brooklyn said, repeating the thought that must have crossed her mind a million times that day after the lawyer had told them about the horse and how they were to care for him.

The horse came with his own social calendar, with dates written in red specifying the times when people had rented out his services for their mares.

The amount of money he got for each "service" made Brooklyn blink, rub her eyes, and think she might have been exaggerating the number of zeros at the end of the number.

She was astounded at what people would pay for a horse. And not to have the horse, just to have the chance of having offspring from the horse.

She had not been able to contain herself and had asked what was so special about the horse. Did his babies come out lined with gold?

The attorney had gone into a short explanation of the value of Nelson, his bloodlines, and the accomplishments that he'd managed to attain in his lifetime.

"There is a website where people can book him, and that will need to be maintained by you or someone you hire. I have the information in this folder as well as the names of the places where he's been advertised. You also have to keep up with the fees for that as well."

There had been a few other things the man had instructed them about the horse. Cormac had cared for horses, as had she, although she'd never owned a stallion before.

He assured them that Nelson was gentle as stallions went, but still a stallion, and would require firm care and strong fences.

"Can you believe about Nelson—"

"What about Nelson—"

They laughed.

"That's been the hardest thing for me to wrap my head around. I know it's kind of crazy for someone to have a child just drop into their life, but I actually was able to adjust to that idea far easier than I was able to adjust to the idea that I own a horse that commands so much money for just a few hours in his presence."

It was a funny way to say stud fees, and Brooklyn laughed.

"Every time he said a child and a horse, it just sounded so...wrong. But Charles and Kendra were looking after us. They wanted to make sure we had the money to raise Quinn. And Nelson was the way they did that. It was actually kind of brilliant if you think about it."

"I knew his family was from a rodeo family, but I didn't know how deeply he was into it. But I guess, as a lawyer, he had extra funds to invest, and instead of doing it in the stock market, he put it into a horse. I think that's probably to our benefit and Quinn's."

"Yeah."

"And I don't know that I want to have my money and your money in our marriage. I think it should be *our* money, but we both have ranches that could use the money, so I feel like we should split the fees until both of our ranches are out of danger. After that, we should be putting some aside for Quinn and her education if she wants or for her to buy a house or whatever she wants to do when she's older."

"That's exactly what I was thinking. I know that the lawyer said specifically that the money was supposed to be for us, not that we had to spend every penny on Quinn. That Charles had been very insistent about that. But I wasn't sure how you felt about it."

"Well, if you disagree, we can talk about it."

"No. I think we will be better off if we don't lose the ranch. We talked about that, and even if things go sideways with Nelson, and we end up losing him anyway, we'll survive. But stability really seems to be what she needs right now."

"I agree."

Quinn stirred, her breath hitching, before she settled back down and started breathing regularly again.

"I guess I could carry her up if it's okay with you. I'm tired and ready to go to bed. I might not fall asleep right away, because there's so much running through my head, but it's been a big day."

"I'm exhausted. I love this time of night, love sitting outside listening to the crickets and feeling the night breeze. So, I wasn't going to say no when you suggested we do it. Plus, I thought it was good for Quinn, and she seems to enjoy sitting on the swing with us okay."

"I think we just need time to settle down and start to get familiar with each other. It's a big change, but we can do it."

He didn't say anything else but stood, careful not to let the swing bounce too much, and went around, putting his arms under Quinn and lifting her up.

Brooklyn walked up and helped settle her into bed, all the while thinking about the fact that she and Cormac were going to be sharing the same room. Such an odd thing. And while she felt comfortable with him, the idea of sharing a room was a little bit disconcerting.

She didn't know exactly what his ideas were, and she wasn't sure exactly how to approach the subject so that they were on the same page. But as he softly closed the door behind Quinn, and they walked side by side to their room, she blurted out, "I was thinking we could sleep in the same bed, just, you know, you on your side and me on mine?"

"That's fine with me. I have a big quilt in the closet I was thinking I could throw on the floor and sleep on it, if sharing a bed wasn't something you wanted to do. I understand if it's not."

"No. I wouldn't want you sleeping on the floor. That wouldn't be right. I can't come into your room after you offered me the guest room and I refused, and then kick you out of your bed. I just... I just want my own side."

"I understand. That's fine."

They didn't say anything more, and by the time Brooklyn had emerged from the bathroom, her dirty clothes in the hamper and her nightgown on, Cormac was already in bed.

And he seemed to be watching her.

"I can move to the other side, I just chose one."

"That's fine. I don't have a preference."

"Tomorrow, we need to go to Rockerton, grab rings, and I know that the pastor wanted us to do our marriage counseling as soon as possible. Jane at the diner has a daughter, and I think there's a little group of girls that run around together, if I am right from seeing it at the church."

"I believe so. There are three little girls. Jane's daughters and some other little girl. They are quite good friends, since they're the only girls their age that live in the town of Sweet Water."

"I was wondering if we could talk to Jane and maybe see what they're doing tomorrow. She might be able to keep an eye on Quinn while we're at counseling since it's Saturday."

"That's a really great idea. That way, she'd have some friends before she has to go to school. I didn't know whether we were going to enter her on Monday or not."

"Let's see how she does tomorrow and Sunday, but if it seems like she's ready, we might as well get her in the routine that she's planning on keeping. Plus, there aren't a whole lot of days of school left this year. She might make a few friends before summer vacation."

"That sounds good. I'm pretty sure Jane has a cooking class for men sometimes on Sunday afternoons. So that might be another opportunity for Quinn to see them, if they hit it off. Or if it doesn't suit them to play tomorrow."

"All right. When I talk to her tomorrow, I'll ask her about the cooking class, and I'll go, just for Quinn."

"Because you don't need to learn to cook?" she asked with a lifted brow.

"That's why I have me a wife, isn't it?" he said, giving his best imitation of a caveman.

"What if your wife can't cook?"

"Oh. I was smarter than that. I found one who can."

They grinned together, and Brooklyn hit the light switch in the bathroom, plunging the room into darkness.

She walked slowly to the bed, lifted the blankets, and slid inside, careful to stay on her side of the bed.

Neither one of them said anything for a few minutes, and he hadn't moved. She pictured him lying there, his head on his hands clasped behind him, staring at the ceiling in the darkness.

She curled up on her side, determined that she would force herself to go to sleep, though she knew that had never worked for her in the past and probably wouldn't work for her tonight either.

After a bit, she said, "Thank you."

Maybe he was asleep and wouldn't hear her. But she just felt she needed to say it.

He moved, like she'd startled him. "For what?"

"For forgiving me for my unkindness to you. For opening up your home to all these new people without a single word of complaint, for acting like it's not inconveniencing you in the slightest to have us all here, for being willing to give up your bed, for being kind, for having integrity and working to do the very best you could with Quinn. That's a start, anyway."

"You know, I wouldn't have guessed any of those things."

"That's a bad habit, isn't it? To say thank you, just blanket it to mean everything. And not really mean thanks for anything. Thanks doesn't really mean much if you don't know what you're being thanked for."

"It definitely means a lot more to me whenever I know what you're thinking, what you're thanking me for. I guess I wouldn't have known if you hadn't said."

"You're right. Another note to myself: he doesn't read my mind."

He huffed out a breath. She was glad she could kind of break the ice between them. They'd been getting along really well, but she still felt a little strange around him. And she assumed he felt the same with her. They hadn't been together long enough for them to be able to anticipate what the other one would do.

Although, she had definitely begun anticipating that he would react appropriately in whatever situation he was in. Appropriately being he would put other people before himself. That's what he had done every time.

She had no reason to think that he would start acting differently at any time.

"I guess if we're doing that, I should thank you for a lot of the same things. Being so kind to Quinn. For being willing to move here. For going along with my suggestion to have Miss Karen move in. I've heard that sometimes having two females in the same house is not a wise idea."

"I've been sharing a home with my sisters for years. I don't think I'm going to have a problem sharing with Miss Karen."

"Thank you for that. Thank you for being willing to bend your life and not demanding that I give in to certain concessions or whatever. Thank you for forgiving me for what you thought I did in high school. Thank you for believing me when I told you I didn't do it."

"I feel bad about that. I'll probably always feel bad about that."

"Don't. I'm not holding it against you. God doesn't either, and I think He worked it out for good." He laughed a little. "Last week this time, did you think you were going to be lying in bed with me? Isn't it funny how things work out?"

"No. I never dreamed such a thing would happen, and yes. It is hilarious the way God sometimes works things out, maybe despite us, and definitely for our good... I feel happy. I'm a little scared, the future is uncertain, I don't know what's going to happen, but there is no doubt I feel happy. And that's mostly because of you."

"I want you to be happy. Thank you for telling me. That actually makes me feel pretty good."

They were silent a little bit more, but this time, the silence didn't feel as stilted. She felt like...maybe, through all of this, they had become friends.

She remembered one thing she wanted to talk to him about. One thing that still had her on edge.

"Cormac?"

"Hmm?"

"Are we still going to do the kissing booth at the summer festival together?"

"What?" he asked, sounding more awake than he had.

"The kissing booth. At the summer festival? It's just a couple of weeks away. I just wondered if we were still doing it."

"I didn't know we were."

"Miss Charlene asked me. I assumed she'd asked you too."

"No. No one said anything to me. That's odd. They do usually pair us up. Just to get a laugh."

"Yeah. I just didn't know how that would affect our relationship. I was a little worried about it."

"I guess you don't need to be. Whoever she had you assigned with isn't me."

He didn't sound very happy about that, and she had to admit she wasn't either.

She was a married woman, and while she hadn't felt all that married earlier, lying in bed with the man made it a little more real. Still, real or not, it didn't matter how she felt. She was married, and she couldn't just go around kissing anyone.

"You want me to take care of that?" Cormac's voice came out of the darkness, startling her. It hadn't even occurred to her that he might do something about that.

She wasn't used to having someone help her with things.

"You probably would have better luck with the ladies than I would. I actually already talked to them, thinking that I would get my name pulled, and somehow it didn't happen." Her words held irony. The ladies had overridden her, quite easily.

"All right. I'll see what I can do."

She thought she'd lie awake for a long time, tossing and turning, because of all the things she had to think about. But that was the last thing she remembered before she drifted off to sleep. Content.

Chapter 18

Sunday morning at church, Cormac dropped his little family off at the sidewalk that led to the door before he continued on to the parking lot.

Last week, he had been a single man with no thought of a family in sight. This week, he had a wife and daughter and...mother-in-law? Grandmother? Whatever he called her. Miss Karen. He had Miss Karen, too.

He would never in a million years have thought that was possible.

It was crazy how life changed so fast, and yet, the change felt right. He certainly didn't think that it was a bad thing. In fact, he thought all the changes were very, very good.

Nelson had arrived with no issues. And he'd spent some time in the early morning strengthening the boards in the corral.

Nelson wouldn't be able to stay in the corral forever, but it would work for now. Because he had wanted to go to Rockerton and get his wife rings.

They'd done that, and he'd talked to Jane. Her daughters had been busy with something at school and couldn't play, but she had said that he should be sure to go to the diner after church for the cooking lessons and to take Quinn with him. She said she would give her daughters some information and encourage them to welcome Quinn to their town, even if she was a little bit younger than they were.

So far on both Friday and Saturday evenings, Miss Karen had gone to bed early, and Quinn had fallen asleep on the swing.

Miss Karen had said the worst time for Quinn was evening when she put her to bed, so having Quinn fall asleep on the swing had been the best thing to keep any homesickness or sadness from happening.

Not that Cormac thought that would be the case forever. Even if she didn't have so much trauma happen in her young life, life was never without its ups and downs.

He appreciated the Lord giving them a few days to get used to each other before whatever drama was going to happen.

The sermon was good, the fellowship sweet, and Brooklyn and Miss Karen strolled to Cassie's house to visit while he and Quinn went on to the diner.

It was close enough that they could walk, so they did. He hadn't been expecting her to take his hand after Brooklyn had told her goodbye, but Quinn had softly slipped her hand into his, and while he hadn't said anything about it, he wrapped his own around hers, content. Smiling inside.

"Do you know these girls?" Quinn asked softly.

"You should have been in Sunday school with them today at church."

"Merritt was the only other girl in my class. There were a couple of boys."

"I think the other two might be a little older. Toni is the name of one, and...Sorrell? Maybe that's the other one's name." He should have found out for sure when he was on the phone with Jane.

They hadn't quite gotten to the door of the diner when three little girls came around the edge of the building, saw them, and ran over to them.

"You must be Quinn!" the tallest one said. She didn't wait for an answer before she went on. "Our mom said that you were coming. She said that we were supposed to play with you. We don't have a problem with that, because we're always looking for new friends. Sweet Water is a small town, and we have to stick together. Mom says that's what makes a community."

Quinn seemed a little overwhelmed with all the talking the girl was doing, and she shrank almost imperceptibly against Cormac's side.

He couldn't believe how protective he felt over the little girl, even though she was only talking to other little girls her age. He wanted to shield her. Wanted to defend her. Make her feel comfortable and be sure that she knew that she was loved.

"Hi. I'm Toni," Toni said, holding out her hand, imitating the adults that she'd seen.

At first, he was afraid that Quinn wasn't going to hold out her hand, and he wasn't sure what to do about that.

But then, slowly, her hand reached out.

"Mom said you might be shy. She said sometimes whenever three people know each other and one person doesn't, one person might feel left out, so we don't want you to feel left out. You want to play with us?" Another little girl, the one that was in the middle for height, spoke. "I'm Sorrell, by the way."

"I'm Quinn." Quinn's words were soft but a little bit more confident than what she had sounded before, and she straightened from against his side, holding her hand out.

They shook, and it was adorable.

Cormac looked away so they didn't see his smile.

"I'm Merritt. We met in Sunday school. And I told you we might be playing together today."

"You did. I liked Sunday school. Our teacher was nice."

"I love her. She's the best. I don't want to move up to Sorrell and Toni's class because I'll miss our teacher."

"Maybe she'll move up with us," Quinn said.

"We can tell her that's what we want her to do," Merritt said.

Sorrell looked at Cormac. "Mr. Cormac, is it okay if we go play behind the diner? Mom always lets us do that while she's teaching her class. Although she's sick today."

"Sure. You can do whatever your mom usually lets you do. Are you okay, Quinn?" he asked, looking at Quinn, wondering how long he was going to be there if there was no class, since Jane was still sick.

He hadn't seen her in church, but honestly he hadn't really been looking. He'd been concerned about Quinn finding her way and about everyone giving Brooklyn and him crazy looks. After all, they were enemies last week, and this week, they were married. It had been the gossip of the century, he was pretty sure, but Brooklyn had seemed to handle it just fine, and it hadn't bothered him at all, but with all that going on, he hadn't thought about Jane.

"Are you going anywhere else? You'll just be inside if I need you?" Quinn asked, already taking a step to go with the girls, then slowing, almost as though she remembered that sometimes people leave and never come back. She hadn't let go of his hand.

His heart went out to her.

"I'll be right inside. I won't go anywhere else without talking to you first, okay?"

She nodded, giving him a little smile, which reassured him a bit, and then her hand slipped out of his, and she ran behind the diner with her friends.

Taking a breath, finding it funny that he found it so hard to let her go, when he barely even knew her, he opened the diner door, listening to the jingle of the bells overhead as he walked in.

"There he is! Miss Jane said you'd be coming, although you're a little late, but you're here!" Marshall, one of the old men who hung out around town with his buddies, Blaze and Junior, greeted him from back in the kitchen area.

"I understand Miss Jane is sick?" he said, stepping in closer to the counter but not bothering to try to go behind. He assumed class was canceled.

"Yeah, she's sick, so I'm in charge of cooking class today. Come on back and we'll get you a hairnet. Unless of course you're allergic to them."

Cormac's brows drew down as he glanced at the man before walking around the counter and going past the area behind it, through the small hall and into the kitchen.

"Allergic to a hairnet?" he asked.

"I have a religious exemption to them," Junior said.

"And I'm allergic to peanuts."

"I see." He looked at the men, then looked around the kitchen. He wasn't sure what to think about the whole hairnet thing, but he finally said, "I might be allergic to them."

"All right then," Marshall said right away. "We wouldn't want to make you wear one." He clapped his hands together. "Class, we're going to begin."

"Stop putting on airs," Blaze said, annoyed.

"She didn't leave you in charge. She left us all in charge. You just volunteered to provide the recipe."

"Yeah. About that. I couldn't find any recipes. I don't know how to get on that dumb TikTok anyway. So, we're just going to have to make something up."

"What? Just make something up?" Junior asked, aghast.

"We're supposed to be serving this to patrons when we open at 6 o'clock. We can't just make something up."

"Sure we can. We just think of things that sound good together, and we'll put them together in a sandwich, and we'll serve that to our patrons. They'll love us. We're going to be a huge success. The only thing that would make this better would be if we had our lady so we could film it and post on TikTok."

"You might want to wait until Jane feels better. Then you won't lose the opportunity to have a video for your TikTok account." Cormac leaned against the counter, his arms folded. This would be interesting, if nothing else.

"Oh, Jane isn't our lady," Marshall said to Cormac, confusing Cormac further. "We don't have a lady yet."

"We don't have one, but we have a plan to get one," Junior added, rather mysteriously.

A plan? Cormac almost laughed. He had had no plans to get a lady and kind of got one dropped on his lap. These four guys didn't seem to be able to find one. He would give them advice, but he had no idea what he had done for God to favor him in such a way.

And, he realized, favor was exactly what he meant, since he couldn't have picked a woman who was better than Brooklyn.

"All right. So we're ready to go?" Cormac said. If he wasn't going to have a cooking lesson, he almost wouldn't have stayed, except for Quinn. But he did have some things he could do at home, including reinforcing the corral boards so Nelson didn't get out, and he wanted to get the show rolling.

"All right, men. We're going to make a sandwich, because that's typical man fare," he said with a little bit of a growl in his voice, and Cormac figured the sandwich might not turn out, but the entertainment was engaging.

"Let's toast it. I like my bread toasted better."

"All right. Let's toast it."

Cormac was happy to know that Marshall was willing to go along with suggestions. That was good. It would have been horrible if the guys had spent the entire time they were concocting their sandwiches arguing about it.

The toaster toasted four slices at one time, so it wasn't any time before they all had their bread toasted.

"All right, the next thing is obviously butter," Marshall said easily.

"Let's do something a little different," Junior suggested. "We don't have to do the same thing that everyone else does."

"We could use mayonnaise?" Cormac suggested. That was his favorite condiment.

"Ketchup," Blaze suggested.

"Let's use peanut butter." Marshall lowered his voice. "The ladies love peanut butter."

Blaze's bushy brows rose, but all the men looked interested. That was all Marshall had to say, and they were searching the kitchen for a jar of peanut butter.

Once they had peanut butter slathered on both sides, Blaze suggested, "Let's put ketchup on it."

"That's disgusting," Junior said.

"We could put mayonnaise on it," Cormac tried again. Peanut butter and mayonnaise was a combination he'd never actually had, but mayonnaise was pretty much good with anything, so he could imagine that it wouldn't be too terrible.

"What do we use when we want to catch flies?" Marshall asked, in a voice that suggested that they actually did want to catch flies. Which, Cormac assumed, they did not.

All three men just looked at Marshall.

"You use honey, not vinegar!" he said, then he laughed at his own joke.

Cormac looked at his sandwich. He didn't really want to ruin the peanut butter and bread by putting honey on it, but no one else dissented, and Marshall started pouring it on his. He assumed that meant everybody else was putting it on theirs.

Jane really ought to be more careful whom she got to substitute for her whenever she wasn't able to take over her cooking class.

"I think we need to give this a little kick. There's too much sugary sweetness here," Blaze said as he looked at the honey glistening on top of his peanut butter.

"A kick as in what?" Cormac asked.

"Chili flakes," Blaze said in a tone that said he thought he was about the smartest man who ever lived.

Cormac couldn't bring himself to argue with that, even though he strongly disagreed. Peanut butter, honey, and now chili flakes? What were they trying to do? Come up with the weirdest ingredients possible?

"That's a brilliant idea!" Marshall said.

At least, as the leader, he was encouraging his class, even if their suggestions were so outlandish that they would never fly for anyone.

But still, Cormac dutifully put his chili flakes on the sandwich, even though he really didn't want to.

"I think we need bacon. Bacon and eggs. Those will be the two final things that will make this sandwich perfect."

Unfortunately, while they were able to find eggs in the refrigerator, there was no bacon.

"But we have this!" Blaze said as Marshall cracked eggs into a bowl to scramble them. Blaze held up a container of imitation bacon bits.

Cormac managed not to throw up, but he wanted to. He hated those things. They didn't have the consistency of bacon, and while they did have the salty flavor, it was a very poor substitute in his opinion.

But the other men didn't seem to hold his high standards for their meal prep, and they nodded eagerly.

Cormac shook the bacon bits on, then he helped Blaze and Junior line up the rest of the stuff on the counter, since they were both convinced that this was going to be the best sandwich that anyone had ever eaten, and they were going to be making a lot of them.

Cormac didn't argue with them. He was pretty sure that people were going to be trying very hard not to puke after tasting the sandwich, but he didn't want to dampen anyone's enthusiasm, and it wasn't a moral issue, so he went along.

After Marshall finished cooking the eggs, he laid a bit of scrambled eggs on top of each man's bacon bits, and then they put the toasted piece of bread on top.

Cormac got a little fancy with his and cut it in a diagonal, while Blaze and Junior cut theirs in half.

Marshall cut the crust off of his.

"Now that I'm living by myself, I don't have to eat the crust if I don't want to," he said simply and threw it in the garbage can.

Cormac knew his grandmother would roll over in her grave if she knew that someone wasted the crust on their bread, but he didn't say anything, pleased with his diagonal pieces. And not minding the crust at all.

"All right, who's going first?" Marshall said as he held up his crustless sandwich.

"We all do it together."

"I agree. If someone's going to die, it ought to be all of us," Cormac muttered and then looked around at three pairs of wide eyes.

"Kidding," he said, holding the hand that wasn't holding half of his sandwich up in the air, in complete innocence.

He was mostly kidding. He didn't really think he was going to die. But he was pretty sure that this was not going to be the best thing he'd ever eaten in his life before. In fact, he felt like it was more likely to be at the bottom of that list.

"All right, boys, on the count of three," Marshall said, holding his sandwich up. "One, two, three," he said, then he looked around as his mouth opened and he put the sandwich in his mouth.

Cormac wasn't going to let the other men do it without him, and he dutifully took a bite of the sandwich, but as he chewed, and chewed, and chewed a little more, he was shocked to find that...he actually liked it. It wasn't too bad. Actually, it was kinda good. No, it was really good. He couldn't believe how good it was.

He had been wrong. As soon as he had swallowed, he said, "I'm shocked. I was not expecting to like it as much as I do, but this is definitely delicious."

He took another bite, just because it really was that good. He had not thought, when he had seen Jane was gone and they were just going to wing it, that he would have anything to bring home to Brooklyn and his family, but this was an easy sandwich that they would really enjoy.

He ate it all, beating the other three men to being done. Possibly because he had more of his teeth, but he didn't make that observation either.

"I think Miss Jane can put that on the menu pretty regular," Blaze said, wiping peanut butter off the side of his lip with the back of his hand.

"I'll tell her she should. I'd buy it. It would go even better with a cup of coffee," Junior said.

"I'm gonna suggest she call it Jaden's Grandmother's Sandwich," Marshall said, and the comment seemed to come out of the blue.

"Who's Jaden?" Junior asked, his eyes scrunched up, suspicious.

"That's my grandson. I'm naming it after my ex-wife, although I'm not using her name, because she's my ex. But she's still his grandmother, so I think it's pretty clever," he said, his posture showing that he actually did find it clever.

"I don't know," Junior said. "It doesn't really seem right that you get to name it after your grandson and your ex-wife."

"I'm not naming it after my ex-wife. It's for my grandson. So the boy knows his gramp created a sandwich."

"Why are you calling it his grandmother's sandwich?" Blaze asked, apparently ignoring the fact that Marshall wasn't the only one who had come up with it. But he was the ringleader.

"Making fun of her a little bit, 'cause this is the kind of thing she would never let me do in the kitchen before, and I feel like I would actually have been a success, if she let me."

Cormac thought about that for a bit. A lot of times, husbands were married to women who didn't support them, and instead of being the success that they could be, they ended up not taking risks that they would like to take because their wives weren't on board with it.

He wasn't sure whether that would happen to him with Brooklyn, but he doubted it would. Maybe she'd just been putting on a show, since they didn't know each other very well, but he suspected that if he wanted to try it, she'd be behind him.

He knew he would do the same for her.

"I don't know about you, boys, but I could go for another," Marshall said, and he reached for the bread.

Chapter 19

"We'll see you later, Quinn. Thanks for playing with us," Sorrell said, watching as their new friend walked away. For a seven-year-old, she wasn't too bad.

But she had a lot of growing up to do.

Sorrell didn't want to talk to the men while Quinn was still there. She was too young. Even Merritt, who was eight, was a little on the young side, but sisters had to be included, because since her mom was sick, she could hardly get rid of hers.

Mr. Marshall, Mr. Blaze, and Mr. Junior had stood behind Mr. Cormac as he picked up his daughter. But now, they walked over to the middle of the vacant lot where Sorrell was playing with Merritt and Toni.

"You girls ready?" Mr. Marshall asked, holding up his phone.

They were going to teach him how to TikTok. As he put it.

"Did you download the app?" Merritt asked, with her brows raised.

"I couldn't figure out how to do it," Mr. Junior said.

"Here. Let me see your phone. I can do this for you, because you'll never have to do it again. But the stuff that you have to do, you're going to have to learn to do on your own, without me doing it for you."

Her voice sounded very authoritative, and Sorrell appreciated it. Even if she was eight, she was the best at the tech part of social media.

Toni took the best pictures and videos. And Sorrell was the best at making captions.

Together, they made a pretty awesome team if she did say so herself.

She kinda felt that the older men were hopeless, but they'd asked if they would help. The men had been so supportive of her mom, and her mom had mentioned over and over again how much she appreciated the men going around town spreading word about the new things that were happening at the diner, and drumming up business for her, that Merritt, Sorrell, and Toni felt like they needed to help out.

That, and the men had promised that they would help them find a dad for themselves. For Merritt and Sorrell for their mom, and Toni for hers.

They all waited while Merritt got the app for Mr. Junior, then got it downloaded.

They couldn't really go ahead without it. Although, Sorrell hadn't figured out whether it would be best for them all to be on the same channel or for them all to have a channel that was similar.

As it was, they set them up on the same channel and emphasized the fact that the men needed to remember their username and password to get in.

Once they were in, it was getting late, and Sorrell said, "We had wanted to show you guys how to upload videos, but it's getting late. And you guys need to get back to the diner, because people are going to be coming in to eat."

The men nodded, knowing that what she said was right.

"Next Sunday, we'll meet at the same place. We'll show you the videos, but you need to be giving us some names." She lowered her brows at them. They had had a deal. The men were helping them find husbands for their moms, and she wasn't going to let them off that easily.

"We're thinking about it. We have a couple of guys in mind, but you can't rush these things. You have to do it nice and slow," Marshall said, making a pushing down motion with his hand to show that they needed to slow down.

"I've been without a father for a really long time, and I've already been nice and slow. I want to move on this." She knew her words sounded very adult-ish, but she wanted him to understand the importance of the situation. She couldn't wait around forever. She was going to be grown up before her mom finally got around to finding a man and getting married and having someone to help raise her.

After all, a girl needed a dad. Didn't she know that?

She crossed her arms over her chest and eyed the men. "We're not going to show you everything next week. We'll only show you the basics. We can't give everything to you without you coming up with a few things for us in return."

"What about the lady? Thought you were going to find us one of those too?"

"We need to get started on TikTok first. Then the ladies will come."

Sorrell was confident about this. She had a plan. One that she was absolutely positive would work, because it worked for other people.

But she wasn't going to tell it to anyone, not even her friends. She didn't want them to be tempted to give out the information and be tricked by the old men. So far, they hadn't come up with anything, and she was still fatherless. As were Merritt and Toni.

"That's a deal. We'll have some names for you by next week, and maybe even some ideas of how to get them together." Mr. Marshall looked at the girls, then solemnly held his hand out.

Sorrell uncrossed her arms and shook, meeting his eyes with a serious gaze of her own.

She was going to get a dad.

Chapter 20

Brooklyn shifted uneasily.

She stood at the kissing booth, waiting. Cormac had tried to get Miss Charlene to give him a definite answer about him being in the booth with Brooklyn, but Miss Charlene had been cagey.

Grandma Karen had Quinn, and Cormac had gone to check with Miss Charlene. Brooklyn figured that he wouldn't allow someone else to be in the booth with her, but all he'd said was, "I'll take care of it."

A line formed along the fence in front of the booth. A few people called out. Someone said they couldn't believe the two former enemies were now married.

They'd had a lot of that over the last few weeks.

They'd also had a lot of time spent getting to know each other and Quinn. A counselor had helped some, but she'd said that Quinn seemed to be doing fine. She'd given them things to watch for and things to talk about, a few assignments to do as a family and had said she'd like to stay out of the picture as much as possible, unless she was needed.

Brooklyn had loved her right away. The counselor had been more interested in helping them forge their family together than in making money for herself. They couldn't have found a better one.

"Miss Charlene had Mr. Marshall scheduled to be in with you." Cormac slipped in the booth beside her, his head leaning down to whisper in her ear.

"Ugh!"

"That's okay. You know that old fellow will do anything for money, so I paid him off."

"You paid him off?"

"Yep. Said I was going to be in the booth with my wife and told him to name his price."

"How much was I worth?"

"I had to mortgage the ranch, but you're all mine tonight."

She laughed, sure he was joking about that, but loving that he made sure they were together. She'd come a long way in her feelings toward him since she'd tried to figure out how to get out of being in the booth with him. Funny that now she wanted to be with him.

Much better than Mr. Marshall.

She'd be kissing her husband.

Kissing him.

The thoughts made her insides shiver, and not in a bad way. Actually, she felt like smiling, because she felt like it was time. They'd been getting to know each other better every day, and if they were really going to stay married, it was time to move on.

She could use logic all she wanted to. The fact of the matter was, she wanted to kiss Cormac. Something she never thought would happen.

"You okay?" he asked, keeping his mouth down by her ear and eliciting shivers again.

"Yes." Could she tell him her shaking was in anticipation? Excitement? And maybe just a little relief?

Music played and the air was filled with the scent of funnel cakes and hot sausage and the laughter and shouts of people enjoying themselves, but she hardly noticed.

She was going to get to kiss her husband. And soon.

He put a hand on her shoulder.

"You're shaking."

She didn't hesitate. "I'm excited."

"Really?" He sounded surprised. "Excited about...kissing me?"

"Yes."

"You want to?"

"Yes."

He blew out a breath, and she would say it was in relief, or maybe disbelief.

"I wasn't sure."

"We didn't really talk about it."

"I was afraid to."

"Afraid of me?"

"No. Just...wasn't sure if you wanted to and didn't want to bring it up, push myself on you – "

"You're my wife. There is no such thing as pushing yourself on me."

"Our marriage wasn't exactly planned or normal."

"But it's going to be real. We decided on that."

"You didn't kiss me."

"I didn't want to push you. I wasn't your favorite person for a long time."

"You and Quinn are my favorite people now."

"That's true. And you kiss Quinn goodnight." There was humor in his tone.

"I think I might want to kiss you a little differently than I kiss her."

"Really? Want to talk about that?" Now he was laughing.

"I think there are people waiting and we probably shouldn't." Of course she didn't want to talk about it! Ugh. The idea.

Of course, with him talking low into her ear like that, his hand lightly stroking her shoulder, his body close, she felt safe and cared for and maybe she could talk to him about the things she'd like to do.

Not here, of course.

"They can wait. I'm talking to my wife, and you're more important than anyone else. I don't care where they are or what they want."

"Quinn?" she reminded him.

"I love Quinn. And any other children we might have."

She could feel her cheeks heating over that.

"But my relationship with you is still more important than my relationship with them. You are the most important person in the world to me. And that will never change."

His words rang with finality.

She hadn't been expecting him to say anything like that and her heart had flipped and her breathing had gotten shallow.

"What have I done to deserve that?" she asked, knowing she didn't deserve it.

"You married me," he said simply.

Disappointment caused her to breathe out slowly, but then he continued.

"But there is so much to admire in you. So much for me to see and thank God over and over that He gave me His very best when he gave me you. You're dedication to Quinn, for one."

"You are just as dedicated. And you opened up your home for us to all move in."

"You all did me a favor. I didn't even realize I was lonely until you all showed up. And I love having a child rattling around the house, but I love even more having you. Just your presence in the house makes it a home for me. I didn't know how much I was missing –"

"Are you guys going to kiss or what?" a voice called.

Cormac kept his head down. "Are you sure you're okay with this?"

"Yes. I didn't have the words to tell you I wanted it. Not necessarily here, but at home."

"You're going to give me a big head. You're also going to make me want to grab your hand and haul you back home with me."

She laughed and he did too, although there was a seriousness in his tone that made her think he wasn't joking.

"We're ready," Cormac called to Roberta, the teen collecting the money.

The girl nodded and said, "We have the first payment. Go ahead."

Cormac jerked his head and looked back at Brooklyn. His hand slid around her and he pulled her close, trembling slightly as her hands slipped around his waist.

He lowered his head and kissed the side of her eye. A feather-soft kiss that took her breath away from the tenderness of it.

"Next!" Roberta called.

His head lowered again and she held her breath as his lips brushed her temple.

"Next!"

His lips gently brushed the bridge of her nose. She closed her eyes.

"Next!"

Another touch, feather soft, at the corner of her other eye.

"Next!"

His mouth lingered on her temple, like he didn't want to move away.

"Next!"

He touched the corner of her mouth.

She wanted to grab him and hold his head and force him to put his lips where she really wanted them, but just as much she wanted to stand still and enjoy being cherished and showered with tender kisses.

"Next!"

His lips brushed the length of her jaw.

She wasn't sure how long that went on, with Cormac fluttering sweet, light kisses on her face and neck, making her fingers tingle and her heart dissolve in a pile of mush. Long enough for her to think that he wasn't ever going to kiss her like she wanted, and long enough for her to quit caring how it was going to look when she grabbed him and held him still so she could kiss him the way she wanted.

Then, his lips hovered over hers, their breath mingled and he moved just slightly and his mouth covered hers, perfect, and exactly what she wanted, even better, although the world spun and she held on tight to him while her heart thundered and her lungs felt like they were fluttering like a trapped butterfly's wings, shallow and fast.

When Cormac finally lifted his head, they stared into each other's eyes. She wasn't sure what he was thinking, but she felt a mixture of surprise and desire to do it all again. Surprise that someone she'd thought of as her enemy for such a long time could make her feel beautiful and desirable and cherished, and she didn't want that feeling to ever end.

"I love you," he breathed.

It was almost too much. The emotions that had been bubbling inside of her seemed to expand to fill up her chest.

"I love you, too." Her words were soft, but came from the depths of her soul. She would spend the rest of her life trying to show him how much she meant those three words.

"I can't wait until this is over," he said softly.

"Tired of kissing me already?" she asked, wanting to say she wanted it to last forever.

"No. I want to take you home where I can do it without an audience."

"Maybe we can stop thinking about our bed as having sides." Hopefully she wasn't rushing things for him, but she'd felt that way for a while.

"I've wanted you on my side for a long time, now."

"I think you should move to my side."

"And we can compromise by snuggling in the middle?"

"Is that what we're going to be doing? Snuggling?"

They grinned, knowledge and anticipation in their gazes.

If Cormac was that good at making her feel like he adored her just by kissing her, she could only imagine how good the rest of their night was going to be.

Enjoy this preview of *Just a Cowboy's Midnight Bride,* just for you!

Just a Cowboy's Midnight Bride

Chapter 1

Mav Stryker stumbled to the kitchen, rubbing his bleary eyes and groping for a coffee cup.

He needed caffeine to soothe the ache and the pounding in his head.

Unfortunately, in the dim glow of the light above the sink, he could see the cupboard was empty.

Rats.

He remembered using his last clean coffee cup two days ago, and yesterday he'd had to rinse one out.

He glanced at the sink. Overflowing with dirty dishes.

Doing dishes was something he hated. Along with cooking. And housework.

He needed a wife.

He'd already tried a maid. She'd quit after one week.

He'd tried a second one, but she must have talked to the first, because she never even showed up for the first day of work.

With one hand pressing against his temple where the throbbing was the worst, he padded to the sink, looking for a cup that would be the easiest to grab and wash.

Both sides of the sink were full to overflowing, so running water over anything would be tricky. But he needed coffee.

Not only for the pounding in his head, but he needed the jolt to jump-start his brain, to check his bank statement, to see that what he had been tossing and turning about all night was not just a bad dream.

Surely it was a bad dream.

The old linoleum on the floor peeled up, and he stumbled as he brought the semi-clean coffee cup to his one-cup dispenser, put it under the drip, and pressed the button to start. He leaned against the chipped, cheap countertop and pulled his phone out of his pajama pocket.

While the coffee dripped, he tried to focus his bleary eyes on his bank app.

Unfortunately, it took less than a minute for him to realize that he had not imagined it. He was almost broke.

The venture he'd invested all of his capital in—crossbreeding Highlander cattle with Herefords—had not panned out the way he had thought it was going to.

He'd overextended his capital and overestimated the profits while underestimating expenses. He hadn't expected last winter to be quite as bad as what it was. Winter in North Dakota was always bad, but it had been an exceptionally hard year, and he'd had to buy more hay than he planned on.

With the fact that he was already upside down, it had left him with next to nothing.

Last month, the mortgage on the farm had pretty much drained him, and then an unexpected illness in his herd, and the subsequent vet bills, had completely wiped him out.

He didn't know what he was going to do.

Maybe dishes and housework weren't the only things he needed a wife for.

He could just hear his sister Lark saying "no wonder you're not married when that's what you think a wife is for." But wasn't that what a wife was supposed to do? Keep the house?

He'd mulled over the biblical commands for a wife and couldn't come to any other conclusion. The woman was supposed to keep the house. That meant doing the dishes, doing the cleaning, and maybe, if he got a really good one, she'd fix some of the stuff that was broken around here, too.

Not that he wouldn't; he just hadn't had time. He'd been working so hard, had sunk everything that he'd made working every job he'd had for more than ten years into buying this spread. Then, he had a tip from an industry insider who'd said Highlander crosses were the next big thing. And when he researched it, the dude had been right. They'd been selling for triple the amount of good Angus beef.

Unfortunately, that must have just been a fluke in the market at the time that he'd researched, because the numbers hadn't held. He'd been waiting, hoping they would go back up, but last spring's calves were ready for market and he wasn't going to get nearly the price he expected for them.

His coffee was done, and he reached around, grabbing it, wincing at the heat, but drinking anyway.

It wasn't going to help him go back to sleep, but it would take his headache away.

His brothers all had money; even Lark, as a vet, would have money he could most likely borrow.

If he understood her correctly, someone had paid for her eight years of schooling, and she had no student debt.

He supposed, as one of her brothers, he should have found out exactly who paid for that school, but the idea hadn't occurred to him until just now, and he dismissed it. He didn't have time to think about that.

He needed to figure out a solution to his problem. And it didn't include going to his brothers. He wasn't going to lose face with them. They already thought he was the flighty one. The one that didn't have a head on his shoulders. No brain. And to a certain extent, they were right.

Maybe part of him not being good with women was because what his brothers thought was somewhat true. That and he was always focused on himself and what the woman he was with could do for him.

That was something Lark had told him once upon a time, and he dismissed it as ridiculous. Now, with his track record bearing witness that there was some kind of issue with him, he probably should give it more credence.

But the most pressing issue was figuring out what to do without telling his brothers. He didn't want them to think he was a failure. Any more than they already did. He was the flighty one. The one who never stuck with anything. Always goofing off. Couldn't concentrate without being distracted by the next shiny thing.

The Hereford-Highlander cross was probably just another in his long string of things that he had gotten distracted with and hadn't worked out.

That's what his brothers would say; he could hear them now.

Of course they would help him. They wouldn't want to see one of their family members lose their farm. They would make fun of him while they did it, though.

He winced again at the bitter brew, slightly less acidic this time than last but still burning his throat as he swallowed.

There had to be a solution.

Why don't you pray?

He believed in God. He would even say he loved God. He was saved for sure, but the God stuff had always seemed a little boring to him.

He hadn't always wanted to do things God's way because he was afraid he might miss something. Might miss out on something fun, or God might tell him to do something like go be a missionary in Africa, which was the very last thing he ever wanted to do.

He'd wanted to have a farm, wanted it to be successful, and he didn't want to spout preacher-ish nonsense to people who weren't interested in hearing it.

To people who were going to hell without someone to tell them the Way.

That little voice in his head seemed to be getting louder and louder. Then of course, it was always right.

Fine. I'll do whatever You want me to do, God, if You just save me from this mess I'm in right now.

He'd made similar promises over the years; a couple of times when he'd been in actual physical danger, he'd prayed that God would save him. After all, he felt like he was too young to die. And he'd said that he would serve God for the rest of his life if God would just get him out of that mess.

He hadn't exactly kept those promises. It wouldn't surprise him at all if God decided to give up on him and not listen to him or help him again.

I'm serious this time. If You help me out of this mess, I'll get serious about reading my Bible. I'll pray. And...

Could he say it? Could he really tell God he would give his life in service to the Lord?

What if God wanted him to become a preacher?

His older brother, Clay, carried the nickname Preacher, not because he was one, but because he had been wise from his youth up.

Mav certainly didn't have any such nickname.

Part of him wished he had. Part of him wanted to be that wise and thoughtful person that everyone went to for advice.

Part of him didn't want to be that boring.

But if he didn't do something, he was going to lose the ranch, and from where he could see, there was no human solution in sight.

He could sell all of his cows, and that would take care of his outstanding bills, but it wouldn't pay his mortgage for the rest of the year, and he would have no income in order to do that. His payment was way too high for him to get a regular job that would do anything more than supplement what he had.

Unless he got a job that paid six figures a year.

That was highly unlikely. All he knew was ranching, a little bit of rodeo, and he'd done ice road trucking in Alaska. But a truck-driving job wouldn't help. After all, it would only supplement his income, but it would take him away from the ranch and keep him from being able to farm full time.

Lord... I will try as hard as I am capable of to live my life for You. I...haven't always been very dependable, and that's probably not going to change overnight, but...I'm willing. I know that's not much, and I don't blame You if You don't do anything, but...it's all I have. You can have me if You want me, Lord. But I wouldn't blame You if You don't. There's not much of worth here.

He didn't admit that to just anyone. In fact, he wouldn't admit it to anyone, other than the Lord.

God didn't need him to admit it. God already knew that a lot of his bluster was just for show. Because he was insecure and felt inferior. After all, all of his brothers were successful. Successful in life, success in farming, successful in their marriages. And here he was, successful at nothing. Not life, not farming—he thought again of his empty bank account—and definitely not in relationships.

Basically, he was a failure, and what in the world would God want to have to do with a failure?

You can continue reading by getting your copy of *Just a Cowboy's Midnight Bride* .

A Gift from Jessie

View this code through your smart phone camera to be taken to a page where you can download a FREE ebook when you sign up to get updates from Jessie Gussman! Find out why people say, "Jessie's is the only newsletter I open and read" and "You make my day brighter. Love, love, love reading your newsletters. I don't know where you find time to write books. You are so busy living life. A true blessing." and "I know from now on that I can't be drinking my morning coffee while reading your newsletter – I laughed so hard I sprayed it out all over the table!"

Claim your free book from Jessie!

Escape to more faith-filled romance series by Jessie Gussman!

The Complete Sweet Water, North Dakota Reading Order:

Series One: Sweet Water Ranch Western Cowboy Romance (11 book series)

Series Two: Coming Home to North Dakota (12 book series)

Series Three: Flyboys of Sweet Briar Ranch in North Dakota (13 book series)

Series Four: Sweet View Ranch Western Cowboy Romance (10 book series)

Spinoffs and More! Additional Series You'll Love:

Jessie's First Series: Sweet Haven Farm (4 book series)

Small-Town Romance: The Baxter Boys (5 book series)

Bad-Boy Sweet Romance: Richmond Rebels Sweet Romance (3 book series)

Sweet Water Spinoff: Cowboy Crossing (9 book series)

Holiday Romance: Cowboy Mountain Christmas (6 book series)

Small Town Romantic Comedy: Good Grief, Idaho (5 book series)

True Stories from Jessie's Farm: Stories from Jessie Gussman's Newsletter (3 book series)

Reader-Favorite! Sweet Beach Romance: Blueberry Beach (8 book series)

Cowboy Mountain Christmas Spinoff: A Heartland Cowboy Christmas (9 book series)

Blueberry Beach Spinoff: Strawberry Sands (10 book series)

Printed in the USA
CPSIA information can be obtained
at www.ICGtesting.com
CBHW071402210524
8814CB00040B/1087